THE HOUSE ON THE HILL.

BY

BERNIE KASHDAN.

Copyrighted Material.

Copyright © Bernie Kashdan 2020.

Bernie Kashdan has asserted her rights under the Copyright, Designs and Patents Act 1988 to be identified as the Author of this work.

This book is a work of fiction and except in the case of historical fact, any resemblance to actual persons, living or dead, is purely coincidental.

All rights reserved. No part of this book may be reproduced or transmitted in any form without written permission of the author, except by a reviewer who may quote brief passages for review purposes only.

Had I the heavens' embroidered cloths,

Enwrought with golden and silver light, the blue and the dim and the dark cloths

Of night and light and the half light,

I would spread the cloths under your feet:

But I, being poor, have only my dreams;

I have spread my dreams under your feet;

Tread softly because you tread on my dreams.

W.B. Yeats- 1865-1939

Chapter 1.

The Airport.

Although the departure lounge was busy, she noticed him immediately. Dark, charismatic, he seemed pre-occupied. Dressed immaculately, Rebecca noticed he held a rugged leather-bound journal in one hand, a beautiful Louis Vuitton briefcase in the other. His jacket looked like Armani, she could tell by the cut, worn with a light blue shirt underneath, dark denim jeans and his shoes... Churches brogues, she was sure. As she was surveying him; he looked directly over at her, catching her gaze. Rebecca felt a hot flush rising, burning her cheeks, and nervously looked down at her "Vogue," palms sweating. This was silly, she was forty years old, for goodness' sake... long past the age of flirtatious glances, though it did feel rather exciting!

"Ladies and Gentlemen, boarding has begun for flight AL62 to Kilmarnock airport, please proceed to the gate with your boarding pass ready for inspection," the agent announced in a curt tone. Rebecca stood up, and as she reached for her Samsonite bag, he was right there, next to her. "May I?" as he picked up her holdall. Oh God, this was ridiculously embarrassing! She mumbled something like: "oh, no need" but, her bag in hand, he stood waiting for her to follow him to the boarding gate. As she walked alongside him, she caught a waft of a cologne she recognised... Hermes? Whatever it was, he smelled divine. He was tall, too, at least six foot. She felt diminutive beside him.

They took their seats, which weren't together fortunately, Rebecca thought. She felt slightly relieved at that. He'd kindly placed her bag in the overhead locker and taken his seat two rows in front.

She felt unsettled about the way he had looked at her, so intently, almost as though he could read her mind! The flight departed, and after they had extinguished the seatbelt sign, he got up and asked if he could join her in the empty seat beside her. She looked up at him, blushing, and said, "Oh…of course, if you like!" nervously.

Rebecca felt awkward, but equally, intrigued. Why would this gorgeous specimen of a male be interested in her? Though careful with her appearance, it was becoming more difficult to do so with age. However, the thought of resorting to cosmetic enhancements was definitely not on the agenda. She was sure about that… she'd seen too many poor examples of it. No, she'd carry on as she was, using the organic skincare brand she loved and had marketed for a living, and taking her hyaluronic acid supplements!

Fortunately, years of practising Pilates and yoga had given her a youthful poise and lithe limbs. She dressed carefully for her age, a bit "rock chick" combined with "classic" (not that Nigel had ever noticed, she had felt invisible to him throughout her miserable marriage.) Rebecca knew how lucky she was to work with a few younger, trendy women, who regularly shared fashion and make-up tips, and provided support for each other through life's trials and tribulations. The regular girls' nights out helped, too!

"Hi, I'm Shaun, Shaun Forsythe." She noticed him glancing at her wedding ring as he reached for her hand. She wished she hadn't worn it... God knew the marriage had been over for years... if it had ever really begun.

Rebecca looked up at him. "Rebecca... Rodgers." She offered her hand towards him. He shook it firmly, holding it for slightly longer than she'd expected.

She was pleased that she'd chosen to wear her "Paige" skinny jeans, "Maje" ruffled blouse and "Essential Antwerp" boots, her current favourite items in her wardrobe. She'd carried her much loved "All Saints" leather and shearling jacket over her arm, and this was now lying over the armrest of the empty seat. He picked it up, folding it, and put it in the overhead locker. "Nice jacket," he said, as his eyes flickered over her, and he lowered himself into the seat beside her. Rebecca was wearing her absolute favourite fragrance too, Byredo's "Slow Dance." The flight attendant stopped beside them with the drinks cart, and Rebecca noticed the pretty blond hostess glancing at Shaun and then winking at her! She felt herself flushing with embarrassment. "Drinks from the bar?" she asked, an Irish lilt to her voice. She giggled with her colleague as Shaun turned back to Rebecca, asking what she would like.

"I'll have a small bottle of prosecco, please." He ordered her one, and a beer for himself.

"There you are, enjoy!" the flight attendant placed the drinks down. As she did so, she whispered "nice after shave" to Shaun! Rebecca felt her cheeks redden as he looked at the young girl, a wry smile on his lips. "Thanks." He muttered.

Rebecca supposed he was used to girls flirting with him, with his chiselled features and piercing blue eyes. Eyes that were, she noticed, framed with thick black lashes. He was gorgeous, no doubt about that. He smelled good too... It was "Terre d'Hermes," she'd recognised it now. One of the sales reps in the office wore it, and she'd always commented on it.

"Where are you headed?" he asked, with a gravelly, subtle Irish accent. Rebecca nervously clutched her hands. She felt as though she couldn't speak! Crazy! She was behaving like a teenager all over again!

"Um, it's a wellness retreat, near Buncragga."

"Oh?" he asked. "Have you been before?"

Rebecca looked at him. "No, not to this spa, but I've been to Ireland many times, I have an aunt over here, she's from Donegal."

"Oh, right? So, how come you are visiting a spa, all on your own?" he asked, inquisitively.

"Well, it's just something I felt I needed to do, at this point in my life." She answered, thinking how ridiculous she sounded. She thought it might make her come across as shallow and self-obsessed, booking herself into a spa. In reality, she'd hit rock bottom in her life, and felt this might offer some gentle healing of mind and body. She'd thought about doing it for long enough... years, in fact!

"I know the place. It used to be an asylum! They've made a pleasant job of doing it up... but why come here, to Ireland, why not somewhere more... exotic?" he asked, a dark eyebrow raised quizzically.

"Oh, well, I love it here... I spent most of my childhood summers visiting my aunt, so I just googled 'Ireland yoga retreat' and this came up first. I really liked the look of it, so I booked it, there and then."

"How long are you here for?" he asked.

"Just four days." Rebecca smiled across at him as she sipped her prosecco.

Descent.

"Ladies and Gentlemen, this is your Captain speaking, we have begun our descent into Kilmarnock airport. Please ensure you fasten your seatbelts now. They must remain fastened until I extinguish the seatbelt signs. Thank you."

Suddenly, the aircraft swiftly began a rapid, steep ascent, its engines roaring thunderously as the overhead lockers rattled and shook. Rebecca looked nervously across at Shaun. The engine noise continued to increase... what was happening? The noises the aircraft was making were terrifying. He reached across, gripping her hand tightly.

"Ladies and Gentlemen, your Captain, please stay calm. We have had to abort our landing into Kilmarnock Airport, because of strong crosswinds. We shall divert the aircraft to another nearby regional airport, and we will keep you updated with those details as they happen. It's a perfectly normal procedure in these circumstances, please remain calm."

"Where do you think we might land instead?" Rebecca asked, feeling slightly awkward that they were holding hands...

"I don't know... it depends on the weather, but don't be afraid. This happens a lot, coming into this airport. It's because it's on a hill, gets all the terrible weather." He stroked her fingers gently, staring at her.

The flight finally landed 25 minutes later, after being buffeted about in the sky for what seemed like an age. The pilot announced the name of the airport, a tiny regional one which was, Shaun told her, only about 20 miles from the "Buncragga Wellness Resort" where Rebecca was going.

As they disembarked, Rebecca saw the pretty flight attendant staring at them and whispering something to a steward who was standing next to her. She felt her cheeks flush again, as the flight attendant gave her a dazzling smile, and said, "Have a lovely stay in Ireland!" The ground staff had arranged a bus back to Kilmarnock airport, and as Rebecca and Shaun left the arrivals hall, they could see a ground agent holding a board up, which said "Kilmarnock Airport Passengers, this way."

"What do you want to do?" he asked.

"Um, not sure, guess I'll get on the transport they've provided?" Rebecca answered, but she knew she didn't really want to do that. She wanted more time with this man!

"We could go together if you like... I'm staying fairly close to there?"

"Well, if you're sure you don't mind? I don't think I could face a coach journey after that!" She said, her nerves still shattered after the flight.

They headed out of the tiny airport to a wooden hut which had a sign advertising a pop-up car hire station. Shaun arranged a four-wheel-drive car, and soon they were heading out of the airport, onto a dark, winding country road. The rain lashed down, obscuring their vision, save for the brief interlude the windscreen wipers provided, as their blades moved back and forwards frantically.

"Jesus, look at this bloody weather!" Shaun complained.

She still felt slightly on edge, but equally excited... God, she'd not felt this giddy in years! What was she doing, getting into a car with a complete stranger whom she knew absolutely nothing about? She tried to stop the worrying voice inside her head and said:

"So, how do you know the place used to be an asylum? That's kind of creeped me out!" Rebecca laughed.

 Shaun laughed. "My aunt worked there for a while, she said it was Godawful. Had been a beautiful hotel way back, but they sold it and that's when it became a hospital. It was a desperate place."

"Oh, so you're from this area?"

"Yes, I am." He replied.

The car's headlights swept around the headland, lighting up the crashing waves visible against the cliffs. "It looks beautiful… wild…" Rebecca murmured.

"Oh, it is." He said, reaching for her hand as though it was the most natural thing in the world to do...

"That's why I'm coming back here..."

"Coming back?" she asked.

"That's for another time." he said, as he looked across at her briefly, before turning back to the wild, windswept road ahead.

Chapter 2.

Dark Rain Organics.

"You must go, Rebecca. It will do wonders for you." Her colleagues Lucy and Mia nodded in unison. "If anything, you should go for longer!" Mia said. "Why don't you speak to Jackie and Alan about taking more time off? It's fairly quiet at the moment, before the pre- Christmas craziness begins." She continued.

"I might, though Nigel will throw a fit if I go for longer and spend more money than I already have!"

"Let him! You need to take care of yourself, it will do you the world of good!" Lucy exclaimed.

Rebecca smiled at them, they were such dear friends. The women had worked together at "Dark Rain Organics" ever since Jackie and Alan had formed the company, launching this headlining new Australian brand of organic skincare in the UK, twelve years ago. Rebecca had been looking for a part-time job, as the boys were six and eight by then. Seeing the administrator position advertised, she'd polished up on her limited knowledge of the brand and applied straightaway...

Successful in her application, she was invited for an interview with Jackie and Alan and offered the job immediately. The hours were great, fitting in around the school run; and the location was perfect, only a short drive to the head office in Richmond. She fell into the role, really enjoying her freedom from the drudgery of her home life. If it hadn't been for the boys, she probably would have walked away from both it, and her marriage, years ago.

Chapter 3.

Buncragga Wellness Resort.

The cedar gates loomed before them "Buncragga Wellness Resort" embossed on them. Shaun reached out of the window to push the intercom buzzer. Opening silently, they revealed a sweeping drive which led up to the front steps of the resort, plane trees lining the way. It had stopped raining, and the stars were appearing in the night sky. Rebecca felt lightheaded, full of... anticipation?

Shaun got Rebecca's bag out of the boot of the car, and walking round, opened her door. "Would you like me to come in with you?" he asked. Rebecca got out of the car, surveying the entrance. She could see that it had been a large, probably very grand hotel, once upon a time, with its long windows and huge cedar front door. Hard to imagine what it might have been like as an asylum, though. Nodding at Shaun, she headed for the steps to the entrance. Shaun took hold of her hand, sending shivers down her spine. He carried her bag up the steps, towards the front door which was slowly opening...

The reception area was completely white, with green ferns either side of the wooden front desk, highly polished parquet flooring and the subtle aroma of bergamot filling the air. Gentle chill out music was just audible. There was a tranquil, welcoming aura to the place.

"Good evening...you must be Mrs. Rodgers? We have been expecting you." Said the gorgeous girl behind the reception desk.

She looked Slovakian or similar, Rebecca thought, with glacial eyes and cheekbones that could cut through an iceberg. She had white blond hair, scraped back off her beautiful face.

Petite, she was wearing a fitted white tunic that accentuated her pert breasts, with "Buncragga Wellness Resort" embroidered on the pocket.

"I am Vanya, pleased to welcome you." She held out a dainty hand, with long crimson nails that matched her full, glossy lips. Rebecca shook her hand.

Rebecca could see that Vanya hadn't even focused on her completely. Her gaze was flitting between herself and Shaun, resting on Shaun's face longer than her own.

"We sent a car for you... but it seems you made your own way?'' said Vanya.

"Were you not made aware they diverted the flight from Kilmarnock? I brought Mrs. Rodgers here." Shaun said, almost dismissive of Vanya. "And she is tired, it was a stressful journey, please show her to her room immediately." He added with authority.

With that, Shaun handed Rebecca a business card, pressing it gently into her hand. "Call me." He murmured as he turned to leave. Vanya lifted her perfectly manicured fingernails to give Rebecca her key-card.

"Louis will show you to your room. Your timetable is on a clipboard, beside your bed, and we have also emailed a copy to you. Room service is available until 11pm, if you are hungry. Sleep well, Mrs. Rodgers, see you in the morning!" Vanya smiled, sweetly. Rebecca looked back out of the front door to see Shaun driving away.

First Night.

Rebecca looked around her room. It was beautiful, exactly as it had looked online. The walls were painted white, and the flooring was highly polished wooden floorboards. An enormous bed was in the centre of the room, made up with crisp white bed linen, huge pillows and a silver fur throw at the end, it looked inviting. It was everything she had hoped for, clean, luxurious and calm. Removing her boots and jacket, she lay back on the king-size bed, as her head sank into the soft pillows. It was comfortable, and she realised how tired she was. Reaching into her jeans pocket for the card he had given her, she looked at the silver wording of it.

SHAUN FORSYTHE AAI

Address TBA

Cell: 0749736601

She ran her fingers over the satin card, remembering his fingers touching hers. AAI? She must look that up. And why no address, she wondered? Feeling aroused as she thought of him, she felt the need to pleasure herself... God, how long had it been? Unzipping her jeans and reaching into her panties, she stroked herself quickly, imagining it was him, looking at her with those intense eyes. She sighed as pleasure overcame her, and she squeezed her thighs tightly together.

Itinerary.

Day 1.

Breakfast: 7-9am

Yoga: 10am

Pilates: 11.30 am

Lunch: 12.30-2pm

Afternoon.

Rest time 2-4pm

Facial   4-5pm

Dinner   7-9pm

Rebecca looked at the timetable. Well, she supposed it was ok but then, she hadn't imagined a gorgeous guy taking over her mind and interfering with it all! She'd booked this "retreat" to carve out some time away from Nigel, not to embark on an affair!

She undressed and stepped into the waterfall shower, and as the powerful jets fell on her, she imagined Shaun caressing her body. Foaming herself gently with the Elemis shower gel, she felt turned on again, just thinking of him. She wrapped herself in the fluffy white bathrobe laid out in the bathroom and brushed her teeth. Looking at her reflection in the enormous mirror, she decided she would call him tomorrow. Rebecca climbed into the crisp bedsheets, exhausted but excited.

She couldn't get Shaun out of her mind! As she made herself comfortable, her silk nightgown gently fell away from her breasts. Imagining him gently prising the ribbon straps down over her shoulders as his tongue flicked over her nipples, she fell asleep.

Nigel.

The house felt empty and quiet without her or the boys. He actually felt something close to pining for them... but no, he wouldn't let that feeling creep over him and take control.

Work as an accountant for a large firm occupied him sufficiently to keep himself busy, and then there were other things to get excited about...

He supposed he should have told Rebecca years ago. But their marriage had been okay, no need to "rock the boat," he told himself. In all fairness, he hadn't really been sure that it was wrong, anyway.

This "retreat" of hers, well, probably long overdue. It would do her good, he supposed. Shame it was costing so damn much! Nigel glanced at himself in the mirror and looked away, embarrassed. He picked up his jacket and left the house, slamming the door behind him.

Chapter 4.

Day 1, Bungragga Wellness Retreat.

Rebecca awoke to the gentle buzz of the alarm on her phone. She felt the most refreshed she had been for a long time, having slept solidly for nine hours! She got up and showered, remembering her decision to call Shaun. God, she felt turned on now, just thinking about him! When she had finished showering and got dressed, she made her way down to the restaurant for breakfast.

There was a vast array of food laid out... fresh fruits, yoghurts, breads of all kinds, pastries... it all looked mouth-watering. She suddenly realised how hungry she was, not having bothered with room service the night before.

Deciding on fruit salad and a croissant, she went and sat at a table by the window.

Looking around the restaurant, she saw three other women sat on their own, having breakfast. Two looked about the same age as her, the third much older. Then she noticed Vanya, standing at the entrance to the dining hall, staring at her. Rebecca felt slightly uncomfortable, but Vanya smiled, walked over, and greeted her. "I am your beauty consultant while you are here with us, and I will give you the most wonderful facial and massage this afternoon."

"Great!" said Rebecca. "I shall look forward to it!" Vanya smiled and flounced off, her white suit clinging to her curvaceous figure.

10am.

Rebecca made her way to the yoga studio, which was in a long, entirely glass fronted room that looked out onto the beautiful grounds beyond, a vast lake in their midst shimmering in the weak morning sunlight.

A solitary crane bent its long neck into the lake, its beak causing ripples to form upon the glasslike surface. Taking her place in front of a yoga mat, Rebecca noticed a wiry Chinese man standing in front of her, hands held as if in prayer. The three women from breakfast came into the room and sat, cross-legged, on their yoga mats. The sound of gentle chanting came from invisible speakers.

"Welcome to Yoga, everybody. My name is Li. We will have an hour of mindful movement, ranging from Vinyasa flow, Yin yoga, and restorative yoga. This session caters for all abilities, with variations for those who wish to take their practice deeper, or easier, as they wish. We will also have 10-15 minutes of Pranayama. This is the practice of moving energy without moving the body. It involves the mechanics of breathing, of the cardiovascular, circulatory, pulmonary, endocrine, digestive and lymphatic system. This practice will help you yield a healthy immune system and resist disease. You will learn, in this breathing session, to gain a calm and clear thought field." He said in a soft, lilting voice.

As she followed Li's calming instructions, Rebecca felt empowered by her movements. She was strong enough to get through this tough time in her life; she was certain of that. After the workout, as they lay in silent relaxation, she let her mind slowly and completely empty.

"That was amazing, wasn't it?" one of the women said to no one in particular. "It was…" said Rebecca. She held out her hand, and the woman shook it gently.

"Ginny" she said, in a crisp British accent.

"Oh hi, I'm Rebecca."

The other two women turned, extending hands to Rebecca and Ginny.

"I'm Sally," said the older of the two, with a broad Northern Ireland accent.

"and I'm Pat" said the third. Rebecca detected a regional accent.

They left the yoga studio together, and went looking for the Pilates one, which turned out to be another vast, glass fronted room, this looking out onto an outdoor pool which was sparkling in the sunlight, surrounded by tastefully landscaped gardens. Rebecca thought to herself she would find out if it was a heated pool, she loved to swim and hadn't had time to for ages. In the studio, the women sat on their mats waiting and chatting amicably until the Pilates instructor arrived. She introduced herself as Linda, and before long she had them all rediscovering their pelvic floors and various other muscles!

Rebecca felt exhausted, and after having had a lunch of heart-warming homemade minestrone soup, she headed back to her room to rest.

As she opened the door and let herself in, she noticed a small package wrapped in silver tissue, a white gossamer bow tied neatly around it, on the side table by her bed. Its tag simply said, "Rebecca, for your room, S." Untying the ribbon, she carefully unwrapped the tissue to reveal a white box embossed with "Diptyque, Negrolis." Opening the box, she saw it was a beautiful candle. Rebecca was surprised, what a lovely thought... how had he guessed she loved candles... particularly this brand? There was even a small packet of matches inside the lid of the box. Lighting it immediately, she inhaled slowly, as the heady fragrance subtly scented the room.

She lay on the bed, reaching beside her to the bedside table for his card. Lifting it to her nose, she could smell leather, freshly laundered clothes, and Hermes after shave. Breathing in the musky, sensuous scent, she picked up her phone and googled 'AAI.'

The search result showed up as "Architects' Association of Ireland." Tapping his number into her phone, she took a deep breath to calm herself.

4pm.

Rebecca headed downstairs to find the beauty rooms, where her facial was to take place... she was looking forward to it. Yoga and Pilates so close together had been intense, and she was aching all over. A back, neck and shoulder massage was just what she needed. Vanya met her at the beauty reception desk and showed her to her private room. As she went in, her eyes adjusted to the darkness in the room, which was lit with subtly scented candles, chill-out music playing softly in the background. Vanya motioned towards the treatment bed.

"Please remove your robe and lie down, cover yourself with the heated blanket so you don't get cold, I shall come back once you are comfortable."

Rebecca did as she was told and lay on the bed, pulling the warm blanket over herself. She felt slightly vulnerable, lying there with only her panties on. It had been such a long time since she'd had any beauty treatments, she'd forgotten what was involved! Vanya gently smoothed her hair away from her forehead, placing a soft hairband around her hairline, and began massaging her face gently, the Elemis oil gently penetrating her skin, as Rebecca felt herself drifting away.

"You have beautiful skin, Mrs. Rodgers,"

"Oh, thank you... I never used to," Rebecca softly said.

"Really? I cannot believe that."

As Vanya's fingers gently massaged her face, shoulders, back and neck, Rebecca imagined Shaun's fingers all over her, and felt a sudden rush of hot wetness between her legs.

"Yes, you do. I have never seen such beautiful skin. What products do you use?" Vanya asked.

Rebecca told her about the organic range that she used, an Australian brand she had worked for since it was first introduced to the UK, twelve years earlier. It had, she said, transformed not only her skin, but thousands of their customers. Then she fell into a relaxed silence, recollecting the conversation she'd had with Shaun.

1.15pm, first day.

"Hello?"

"It's Rebecca… thank you for the beautiful candle… it is alight beside me."

"Ah, well, I thought it may be of some comfort to you in that bleak place!"

"It's not bleak… I really rather like it."

"How was your night?" he asked, softly.

"Lovely, the bed is so comfortable… I slept for nine hours! "

"I would have liked to be there, beside you…" Shaun said. She felt herself blushing, he was openly flirting with her and she wasn't sure how to respond! Then he said:

"Can I come and collect you... take you out for dinner?"

"Okay... that would be lovely..."

"What time?'

"7 pm."

"Mrs Rodgers!" Rebecca looked across the lobby at Vanya. "Where are you going?" she asked.

"I'm just meeting my friend for dinner!" Rebecca exclaimed.

Vanya raised an eyebrow, "you must rest!" she exclaimed.

Rebecca smiled and waved her goodbye, as Shaun drove off down the long drive in the car he had brought her here in... yesterday! It already felt like ages ago!

The restaurant was intimate and quiet, as they sat down at a table by a small window which looked out across the bay. Lights on the many boats that were moored up twinkled, and a bright moon was shining, lighting up the calm waters with a silvery gleam. The night sky displayed a dazzling array of stars, a completely different scene from the evening before, a peaceful night with no wind or rain.

"Would you like wine?" Shaun asked.

"White, please... a Sauvignon?" Rebecca said.

A pretty, dark- haired waitress came over, lighting a tea light and placing it on the table with two menus.

"Good evening, Shaun! It's been a wee while since we saw youse!" she said, chirpily.

"It has, Eileen. This is my friend, Rebecca."

"Pleased to meet you! And how is the house coming along?" she asked, as she looked at Shaun appraisingly.

"Very well... almost finished. Now, could we have a bottle of the 'Oyster Bay', please?"

"Of course, I'll fetch that for youse."

He looked across the table at Rebecca, his blue eyes piercing, and she felt the same rush she had felt before when he looked at her that way.

"You are beautiful," he whispered.

She looked down at her hands, blushing, and he reached for them, "now you look even more beautiful."

Eileen brought the wine with two chilled glasses and poured them each one.

"Just to let you know, we have lobster Thermidor on the menu as our special tonight besides the catch of the day, which is wild salmon." she added.

"Thank you, we'll decide in a while." Shaun said.

Rebecca smiled at the way he charmingly dismissed these girls! He made her feel he literally only had eyes for her. Sipping her wine, she tasted the delicious, crisp flavours of her favourite label on her tongue. The menu was delightful, with fresh scallops, mussels, oysters... all Rebecca's most-liked things to eat. She decided on the scallops to start, followed by the Thermidor, realising she was ravenous.

"It's all locally caught," Eileen explained to Rebecca as she took her order, followed by Shaun's.

"Thank you, Eileen. I'm really looking forward to it!" Rebecca said.

"So, tell me about you, Rebecca." He looked at her with intensity, when Eileen had gone off with their order.

She felt awkward, unsure what to say. He reached and took her hand again, stroking her fingers gently. "Don't be afraid. I want to know everything there is to know about you." He whispered.

Chapter 5.

Rebecca.

"I married Nigel when I was nineteen… he was my first proper boyfriend. It was only a short time after we got married that I found out he had a violent, aggressive streak. I was scared of him, but I accepted it, thought that was normal, that most men were like that. I became pregnant with James almost right away.

Poor James had a hard time with Nigel, he punished him for everything he did. When James was a few months old, I decided to leave him, but the day I finally plucked up the courage to, with my bags packed and a temporary stay at my sisters' place arranged, Nigel arrived home early from work, and when he saw we were leaving, he became incandescent with rage.

He pulled poor James out of my arms, shoved him roughly into his car seat in the kitchen. Then he forced himself on me, violently, right there on the floor. Sam was born nine months later, and then I had to stay put.

I stayed with him, because I had nowhere to go. Andrea couldn't help indefinitely, she had just had a baby of her own. Our parents had moved to the South of France shortly after I'd got married. It had always been their dream, and Dad could take early retirement from his job, so they upped and went. We were glad for them, Dad had worked abroad for years, and Mum had practically brought us up on her own, so we felt it was the right time for them to move on.

So, we existed. Nigel became easier to tolerate, should I say, when Sam was born. We just existed. It was better when I started working again; I had money and more freedom from the constraints he put upon me. I saw more of my friends, less of him.

When we went to France in the school holidays Nigel rarely joined us, he was always working. And now the boys have left home, gone to uni, and I'm alone with a husband I barely speak to... who I can't stand.

That's why I came over here... to have time away from the house, from him, try, and decide what I am going to do with the rest of my life, before it's too late. But really, I don't know."

She looked across the table at Shaun, as tears welled in her eyes. She hadn't talked so openly with anyone, ever, about Nigel, apart from Andrea.

Nigel.

Bitch hadn't rung him, again. Probably wasting money on a salt scrub or something ridiculous. God, if she were at home, he'd show her what for! A good fuck would teach her! He dialled her mobile for the umpteenth time that day. Straight to answerphone. Bitch! He glared at himself in the hall mirror, smoothed his receding hair down, and left the house, slamming the front door shut behind him.

Shaun.

He took her hand, gently stroking it.

"You should have left him, but I understand why you felt you couldn't."

She looked back at him, at those gorgeous, piercing blue eyes.

"I know, but I just wasn't able to find the courage to, and I stayed for the boys' sake." she whispered. "It became easier to put up with the status quo than think of a future alone, with two young children. And anyway, he would have prevented me from leaving, somehow. I know that."

"What about you... are you married?" she asked, almost afraid of the answer.

"Once, I was. No children, though."

The food arrived, and as they ate, he told her about the local area, trying to lighten the conversation. Before she knew it, two hours had gone by, and she realised how exhausted she was. They strolled back to the car, holding hands as though they'd been lovers for years.

Bungragga Wellness Resort.

He drove up the long winding drive, still holding her hand and caressing her fingers. She felt totally at ease with him as she looked across at him, this gorgeous man. The car slowed to a halt, and then she felt his lips upon hers, gentle, searching, then more vigorous, as she responded, closing her eyes. The kiss seemed to go on forever, his tongue reaching into her mouth, deeply and tenderly...he pulled away, looking deeply into her eyes.

"Rebecca, I want to be with you." he said.

Chapter 6.

Day 2.

Rebecca woke up after the second night's deepest sleep she'd had for such a long time. She'd had intense, erotic dreams; she felt almost embarrassed. Remembering the passionate kiss they'd shared, she showered and applied her makeup. Running her tongue along her lips, she could almost still taste him. Sighing with pleasure, she got dressed, ready for her next yoga class.

Today's itinerary was for Yoga at 10am, Pilates at 11.30, lunch at 1pm, the same as the previous day. She headed down for breakfast, and as she entered the dining room, Ginny waved across at her, so Rebecca went over to join her.

"Morning" she said breathlessly, as she sat down at Ginny's table.

"We didn't see you at dinner last night?" Ginny said. Rebecca felt herself blushing. "I had dinner out... with a friend." She replied.

"Oh, someone from this area?"

"Well, yes, kind of." Rebecca wished she hadn't sat with her now. Questions were not what she needed! She quickly changed the subject, then excused herself as she went to see what delights today's buffet held.

After breakfast Rebecca went back to her room and brushed her teeth. Her phone pinged with a text message from Shaun.

"Good morning, darling. Can we see each other again tonight? I miss you. xx

In the studio, Li appeared, rolling out mats and lighting the aromatherapy candles around the room.

"Good morning! Good morning!" he nodded at Rebecca and the others.

Lying on her mat with her eyes closed she took a deep breath, inhaling the subtle scent of bergamot. She thought about Shaun's lips on hers, the taste of him, the smell of him. God, it felt so right. She couldn't believe she had only just met him, she felt safe, and so comfortable with him.

The gentle music started, and Li murmured "Namaste." After a gentle tai chi warm up of deep stretches, he took them into the vinyasa flow. Rebecca felt strong, as though she could take on the world. It would all be ok, she told herself.

2pm.

Her phone buzzed beside her as she napped. She woke suddenly, remembering she hadn't replied to Shaun's text!

"Did you get my text? Can I see you tonight?" he said.

"Oh, I'm sorry! I meant to reply, I would like that very much. Same sort of time?"

7pm.

Shaun's car drove slowly up the long drive. She slid into the leather seat beside him, and he reached for her hand. Noticing Pat, Sally and Ginny looking directly at them, out of the dining-room windows, she looked away.

"It seems you have an audience?" he remarked, as he sped out of the drive.

Shaun parked at a tiny cottage pub called "The Rising Tide," which overlooked the bay. As they walked towards the front door, the smell of burning peat filled the air. "C'mon inside," he said, as he grabbed her hand. Locals sitting at the bar winked at them in a welcoming way, as they entered the pub. They sat, drank wine and Guinness, ate fresh sardines, mussels, and whelks, to start, followed by bowls of hearty Irish stew. He asked her about the spa, and what she thought of it.

She made him laugh, telling him about some unusual yoga positions they'd had to put themselves into, and about the three nosey women and their questions. Completely at ease, it was as though they'd known each other for years. The fire cackled and spat in the hearth, and she didn't want the evening to end.

A couple of hours later, Shaun drove back to the resort, and parked away from the main entrance. Turning to her, he cupped her face as he leant in to kiss her.

Day 3.

Vanya was cross. "Mrs. Roberts, you are not taking this programme seriously! You should not leave this place! You must rest!"

"Vanya, I have paid rather a lot to be here. So, if I choose to leave the premises, I think that's up to me!"

Vanya turned away, embarrassed, her pretty face flushed.

10.00am. Yoga.

The three women glanced at her as she entered the studio.

"Morning!" Rebecca said, smiling.

"Morning... who is this rather dashing chap you've been meeting? He looks vaguely familiar..." asked Pat.

"Well, actually we met on the flight over here..." Rebecca answered.

"Oh, tell!" asked Ginny. "We'd all love to meet someone else other than our husbands!! Why do you think we're here! Although not much chance of it..." She said, looking around at the empty studio.

Li began the class. Deeply restorative moves flowed for the next hour, and finally it was time for the relaxing Pranayama. As the meditation began, Rebecca decided she didn't really want to tell these interfering women anything!

She inhaled deeply, as instructed, remembering Shaun's lips on hers. God, she'd never known kisses could be like that. She knew now that she'd never been kissed properly, and certainly never by Nigel. She shuddered at the thought of his sloppy, wet mouth.

"Namaste" Li murmured. The relaxation was over. She quickly slipped out of the studio to avoid any idle chat with the three nosy women.

As Rebecca surveyed the buffet lunch, sumptuous artisan cheeses, hams, chorizos, salads and breads, Pat appeared, right behind her.

"So, who is this gorgeous man of yours?"

Rebecca turned to look at her directly. "He's called Shaun. We've only just met..."

Pat raised an eyebrow, "so you don't really know anything about him?" She said, almost disapprovingly. "What's his surname?"

"Forsythe... why?"

"Well, he looks familiar. Is he from these parts?"

"He is." Rebecca replied, turning back to the buffet and helping herself to lunch.

4pm.

Rebecca's phone buzzed, waking her from a deeply relaxing sleep.

"Can I pick you up soon? I want to take you somewhere." Shaun asked.

"Ok, I will be ready at 5!" she replied.

She slid into the passenger seat as he reached across and kissed her hand. "I've missed you" he whispered, leaning across and brushing his lips against hers. Feeling the familiar stirring between her legs, she smiled. "I've missed you too."

The Caves.

Shaun drove down the road slowly, carefully negotiating the steep bends and inclines. The weather was fair, cold but bright. As he took the left fork into a narrow lane that headed towards the sea, Rebecca looked at the view before her. The Atlantic stretched out in front of them, beyond a vast expanse of white sand dunes. "This is amazing...where are we?"

He parked in a rocky layby between two enormous boulders, and gently taking hold of her hand, led her down an uneven path to the dunes, the wind whispering around them. They followed a wooden slatted path down towards the beach, the spiky marram grass that grew so profusely here poking between the slats.

"This is Lough Rosslaire" he said, "the place I love most in the world."

They carried on walking towards the sea, as the Atlantic waves crashed and rolled in noisily before them. As they walked, the caves came into sight, huge craggy black rock formations that jutted skywards from the white sand. They carried on towards them and as he led her inside the first of the cavernous caves; the air became chilly and damp, the smell of sea-spray and seaweed filling her nostrils.

   Standing still for a while, they took in in the sheer awesomeness of the cave. She shivered as Shaun turned towards her, cupping her face in his hands. He leant in further, his tongue gently probing her lips, then sucking and licking them, gently… she could taste the salt of the ocean on his. Rebecca felt faint as she leant back into the wall of the cave, Shaun pressing himself against her. She could feel his hardness against her thighs, as the waves boomed in the background and the light faded.

"I wanted to share the magic of this place with you." he said, as he held her tightly. Rebecca murmured how beautiful it was, as his lips continued their searching…

"I would love to see this again…" she whispered breathlessly.

"You will, I promise." He replied, his hands in her hair, his lips against hers.

"Will you have dinner with me?" he asked, as they walked back to the car. Rebecca saw it was past seven, and her stomach was growling.

"I'd love to... but I'm paying!"

"I won't hear of it!" He put his arm around her shoulders and pulled her closer.

Shaun parked up at the port, it's pretty streetlamps aglow and the smell of freshly cooked seafood filling the air. They walked along the front until they came to a little restaurant called "The Lobster Pot."

It was a tiny, rustic place with about ten tables, red and white checked cloths on them, glass jars with lit candles on each one. Cosy and intimate, the fire was lit in the hearth, and they sat at a small table next to it.

They ordered a lobster paella to share and drank pints of Guinness, something Rebecca had never tried before. Shaun took hold of her hand and told her about his plans to leave England and come back to Ireland, here to his hometown. He had left Ireland when he was just eighteen, to study architecture first in Paris, then London. Then he told her about his ex-wife.

"A colleague introduced us, he thought I should put an end to my bachelor status. Renee was a fashion designer, absolutely obsessed with the rag trade. We were good, at first, but we got married far too quickly, and it didn't take long to realise we had absolutely nothing in common.

We didn't make each other happy in the few years we were together. It was such an artificial existence, endless rounds of shows and parties, full of fake people. She loved the whole aspect of living that life, but I quickly grew tired of it.

So, I threw myself into my work; concentrating on a contract to redesign an ageing hotel in the West End. That took a couple of years, by which time we'd completely grown apart. I think it relieved her when I suggested we should part ways. Later, I found out she'd been seeing another guy for some time, anyway.

I moved out of the flat we rented in Westbourne Grove, found another place in Islington. That's where my things are now until I leave London. I first came back over here three years ago and started the planning of the house I've had built. I'd always known I would come back here to live, I just didn't know when.

The divorce and charade of London life made my mind up for me. I'm a self-employed architect, so it will be easy enough for me to find work here. A job

I'm on needs finishing in London, so I'll probably keep the place in Islington till that's done, then I'm coming back here for good."

Rebecca listened intently as he talked, loving the Irish lilt in his deep voice, and wishing she had met him years ago. After they had eaten, Shaun drove her back to Buncragga. As he pulled up in front of reception, he looked deeply into her eyes, as he said:

"I don't want you to leave."

Chapter 7.

Day 4.

"Mrs Rodgers! This is the most important day of your retreat! Where have you been?" Vanya scolded her. Rebecca apologised for being late for her full body massage, after the most punishing yoga class yet.

"Vanya, please don't scold me." she said, teasingly. "I have had the most amazing experience here, don't spoil it for me!"

"I'm sorry, I did not mean to offend you." Vanya said, as she gently began Rebecca's 45minute full body massage...

Her fingers kneaded, then stroked, then kneaded, using a warm, deliciously scented oil. Rebecca felt herself becoming aroused with Vanya's strong but sensual touch, massaging then stroking. She placed hot stones on her back, and Rebecca felt herself drifting away, as Vanya's hands moved down to work their magic on her legs.

4pm.

She got back to her room, slipped off the robe Vanya had given her, and lay down on the bed. Within seconds, she was in a deep sleep.

Vanya's crimson lips were on hers gently kissing her, breathing down her neck towards her bare breasts and licking her nipples, flicking her hard tongue over each one. Rebecca groaned, arching her pelvis, wanting more. Vanya slowly moved down towards her silk panties, which she gently pulled to the side as her tongue travelled further, softly teasing and licking, as Rebecca shuddered and came. She jolted awake, breathless. She had dreamt Vanya was making love to her! My God! What was happening to her!

Lifting herself up off the bed, she took off her soaked pants and stepped into the waterfall shower, delighting in the stream of aerated water falling on her. Wrapping herself in the fluffy bathrobe, she lit the candle Shaun had given her, and inhaled deeply as its beautiful scent subtly filled the room.

Shaun was picking her up at 6pm on this, her last evening here. After breakfast tomorrow, she was due to leave. She realised she didn't want to go back to her empty life with Nigel. How could she go? How could she stay?

   Wanting to look her best this evening, she dressed carefully. Shaun had said he had something special he wanted her to see. Choosing her charcoal grey cashmere knit, with her

All-Saints black jeans and her biker boots, he'd said to wrap up warm, so she grabbed her cashmere scarf and the leather jacket he had admired on the plane. She sprayed her favourite perfume on her pulse points, applied a touch of nude gloss to her lips, and headed down to meet him.
Fortunately, Vanya was not around, she felt embarrassed by her dream! Rebecca climbed into the passenger seat and Shaun leant towards her, breathing her scent in and gently kissing her.

"God, I love the scent of you! What is it?" He asked, taking her hand and slowly driving out down the long drive.

"It's called 'Slow Dance,' by Byredo… I got it in Liberty's, smelt it and fell in love with it!"

"I've fallen in love with it!" He smiled across at her.

"Where are we going?" She asked.

"Home," he replied.

The House.

Shaun took the same road as the day before, towards Lough Rosslaire, but this time, he didn't park in the rocky layby. He turned left up a long, narrow, winding lane. As he reached the end, an amazing oak and glass two storey structure appeared before them, its glass front reaching from the ground right up towards the slate tiled roof. It was stunning. As they approached, lights illuminated all around the house, giving it an ethereal feel.

"Oh, my goodness, is this your house?" Rebecca whispered.

"This is it. Come on, let me show you."

They got out of the car, and he led her by the hand up towards the gigantic oak front door, with its glass panels on either side. Olive standard trees in huge terracotta urns stood either side of the white gravel path that led to the door. He unlocked it and, silencing the alarm that fired into action, let them both in. As he flicked a light switch, the vaulted hallway slowly lit up, ambient mood lighting distributed from a trio of enormous hanging amber orb lights.

The wide hallway was dominated by a huge oak staircase with glass panelling at the sides, all the way to the top. The grey slate floor tiles complemented the oak beautifully. Rebecca followed him up the stairs to spacious landing, and then they just stood, staring at the views through the vast front windows. In the twilight, she could just make out the beach beyond, with the huge black caves to the left and the Atlantic in the distance.

"Oh my God, this is simply stunning. Is it all your own design?"

"Yes, it is all mine." He said, as he leant towards her to kiss her.

He showed her around the upstairs, which was completely unfurnished. There were two huge open plan bedrooms with en-suite walk-in showers. Each had magnificent views: towards the mountains on one side; the sea on the other, through long gallery windows.

There was an enormous bathroom between the two rooms, this with a view of the mountains through its panoramic window. A large roll top bath was in the middle of the room, the floor laid with black-and-white marble tiles.

As they made their way downstairs, Rebecca asked him what had inspired him for the design of the house.

"The sea, the caves, the view... I had it all planned. My father had this plot of land for years, used it for his sheep. I used to come up here with him as a boy, and we would sit and look at the view, eating our sandwiches. That's when I fell in love with it. He left it to me, when he died, a few years ago now. My Mam had gone not long before him, and I think he died of a broken heart. So, as my relationship with Renee failed, I made this happen. It's taken three years to complete, but it's almost there now."

Downstairs, Shaun led her into the lounge with its panoramic sea view, and centrally located fire pit. Similar orb lights hung from the high ceiling, this time in smoky grey glass. This room too was an open plan design, the dining area towards the rear, looking out to the mountains. Oak concertina doors led through to a vast kitchen, with floor to ceiling cabinets in a dove grey finish, which complemented the slate floor perfectly.

In the middle of the kitchen there was a large cooking island, with butler sinks either side of it. To the side of the room, the window looked out to the sea at the front, and glass doors at the back opened out to the mountains. It was, Rebecca said, the kitchen... no, the house... of dreams! He pulled her towards him, kissing her with such passion she felt delirious.

"You like it, then?" He said, his breath warm against her cheek.

"I love it. When do you think you'll move in?" she asked him.

"I've yet to furnish the place, as you can see, but I'm hoping in the next few weeks" he replied, gazing at her with such longing she felt weak at the knees.

"Have you decided on a name for it, yet?"

"I have, it's 'Teach an Tobar,' which is Gaelic for 'The house on the hill.'" He led her out of the house, back to the car, and for a moment they just stood, holding hands, gazing at the view before them, now bathed in moonlight. After a while, Shaun drove back to the port and they went into the first restaurant he'd taken her to. Eileen winked at them as they walked in.

"Lovely to see youse again!" she exclaimed.

Shaun ordered drinks, and they sat in comfortable silence, just looking at each other.

"Don't go back." he whispered.

She felt tears welling up again. He reached across and gently brushed them away.

"You can stay with me, for now, at my rented place? And then…"

"I can't, Shaun. I'm afraid what he will do to me!"

"Rebecca, you can't live in fear. You can't waste your life. I... I have fallen in love with you. I want to care for you, protect you..."

"Oh my God, Shaun, I've fallen in love with you, too" She whispered, as the tears rolled down her cheeks.

"Now I hope the wine wasn't that bad?" Eileen asked, as she appeared with tissues, handing them to Rebecca.

Buncragga Wellness Retreat.

10 pm.

"I'll wait here for you, be quick!" Shaun said, squeezing her hand.

Rebecca ran in, relieved Vanya was not there, waiting to chastise her. Louis greeted her as she went up to the front desk.

"Hi Louis, um, I'm leaving tonight, rather than tomorrow. Please, can you prepare my final bill? I'm just going up to collect my things!"

Rebecca ran to her room and hastily bundled her belongings into her bag, not forgetting the gorgeous candle Shaun had given her. She quickly checked the room and the bathroom and, closing the door quietly, headed back down to reception.

"Sorry to see you go, Mrs. Rodgers!" Louis said, as he handed her an invoice. Checking through it quickly, she handed him her credit card, which he swiped and returned to her.

"Please do leave a review, now!"

"Thank you, Louis, I shall. It has been... unforgettable!"

She stepped outside the front door and, taking a deep breath, walked to the car without looking back.

10.45pm.

Shaun parked the car outside the white-washed cottage he was staying in just outside the port. Opening the front door for her, he let her in. Inside, it was basic but warm, embers still glowing in the fireplace. He led her into a small kitchen furnished simply with a fridge, cooker and table and chairs. After showing her the bathroom, he led her into the only bedroom which simply had an enormous brass bed in it, all but filling the room.

He gently eased her jacket off her shoulders and bent his head, kissing her neck, her throat, inhaling the heady scent of her. Lifting her hair up with both hands, he looked at her, his eyes piercing into her. Rebecca pulled him towards her, her lips quivering with desire.

He lifted her up, carrying her to the bed and laying her across it, as he lowered himself on to her. This kiss was the most passionate one yet, his tongue deep in her mouth, searching, probing, as she responded. It seemed to go on forever, as she felt his breathing intensify, her own coming in sudden gasps of pleasure and arousal. "God, I want you so much, darling. Can we make love?" He asked. She nodded, smiling. He got up, helping her as she kicked her boots off. He undid his shirt, throwing it off to reveal a tanned, lean torso with fine, black hair covering his chest. She looked up at him. "Yes indeed, we can..."

Shaun closed the bedroom door, dimmed the light and lay down next to her, resting on one arm. He lifted her jumper, pulling it gently over her head, and slipped her bra straps down, leaving just the sheer, nude lace covering her breasts. He leaned across, his lips brushing her nipples through the lace. His tongue circled them, at first slowly, then more quickly, then slowly again. Rebecca felt her back arch as she breathed softly, whispering his name. His tongue moved down her body as he deftly undid her belt and unzipped her jeans. He pulled them down off her, looking at her intently as his tongue carried on down her body, kissing then licking her as she moaned and writhed against him. He slipped her nude lace knickers down. Feeling herself becoming wetter and wetter as his tongue moved more quickly on her, suddenly she felt herself coming, shuddering beneath his lips. He stood up, and, removing his jeans quickly, whispered "are you sure, darling?"

She pulled him back down to her, slipping his shorts off, gasping at the sight of his manhood as she took him in her mouth. His hard cock filled her mouth as she stroked and cupped his balls. He lifted himself up, "Rebecca, I have condoms?"

"There's no need, I had a hysterectomy a few years ago..." she whispered.

He eased himself down next to her, teasing her panties fully off and pulling her astride him as he entered her slowly. She threw her head back and started moving on him, rhythmically, back and forth. He grabbed her hips, thrusting into her, all the time looking at her.

"God, you are so beautiful. Your breasts… your body… you taste beautiful…" Shaun gazed at her, pulling her down to him so he could suck her nipples as they came together, a crashing climax as he ejaculated in her and she collapsed onto him.

12.30am.

She lay in his arms, spent and exhausted. He stroked her head, looking down at her. "I am completely in love with you, you know, Rebecca." She felt tears pricking her eyes again as she looked into his, whispering, "I love you, too, Shaun."

Day 5.

The sunlight filtered through the faded floral curtains, waking Rebecca from a deep, dreamless sleep. Shaun was already awake, lying next to her as he looked at her. "Good morning, beautiful, how did you sleep?" He leaned across, kissing her softly on her lips, shoulders, fingers.

"Really well." She smiled, suddenly feeling self-conscious. "You are amazing, darling," he whispered, as pulled her tightly closer. Her phone buzzed on the bedside table, and as she looked at it, she saw it was Nigel. There were several missed calls from him, too.

"Oh God, what am I going to do?" she murmured, hiding her face with her hands.

"Leave it for now, we can talk over breakfast."

Shaun cooked breakfast, proper Irish bacon and scrambled eggs with soda bread, and he made them strong mugs of tea. They sat at the little table and ate, as Rebecca remembered they hadn't had dinner the night before. They had left the restaurant without eating in the rush to get her things from the resort.

"This is fabulous!" she exclaimed, as she ate hungrily.

"So, will you stay? While we decide things?" he asked. She looked at him, slowly nodding.

Nigel.

He had tried her number four times… still no answer. He kicked a chair out of the way and tried it again. It was 11am.

"Nigel?"

"Where the hell have you been! I've called you umpteen times, you selfish cow! How dare you not answer? Where

are you? You are supposed to be back today!"

Shaun raised an eyebrow, able to hear Nigel shouting down the line. Rebecca let him rant on for a bit, then quietly said:

"I'm not coming back. I'm leaving you, Nigel."

"What! are you out of your mind? Has that place made you take leave of your senses? You get back here right now or..."

Rebecca hung up. Nigel called her back immediately, cursing as it went to answerphone. He threw his phone at the wall, pacing up and down, his face becoming redder and redder. His phone beeped, and as he picked it up off the floor, he saw her text message.

"You will hear from my solicitor. I am divorcing you on the grounds of

unreasonable behaviour. I am never coming back."

Buncragga Wellness Resort.

Pat and Ginny sat in the dining room, having breakfast together.

"I wonder where Rebecca is this morning?" said Ginny.

"Well, I heard a car late last night, so naturally I got up to look out of my window because the engine was running for a bit, and eventually I saw her getting into it! With her suitcase! That chap she's been seeing since she got here was at the wheel. I saw her kiss him! And he just looked so familiar to me again, even though it was dark, so I googled him this morning. Well, he's only Shaun Forsythe, the famous architect! He won the Royal Institute of the Architects of Ireland award last year, I saw it on the news. He's really quite famous here, you know!" said Pat, excitedly.

"Ooh! She never let on! So, she's left with him, then? I knew today was her last day! Wonder where they've gone? And what about her poor hubby?" Ginny replied.

Rebecca held the phone, shaking, as Shaun hugged her tightly. "Come, let's go out, get some fresh air, talk about things?" he said. She showered in the tiny bathroom, and as she got ready, thought about her next move. First, she would email their solicitor, Susan Clark, and ask her to start divorce proceedings against Nigel. Then she must ring the boys later and talk to them. She couldn't see any further than that at the moment. It struck her just how easy it had been to make the decision that would change her life, forever.

They got in the car and drove to Lough Rosslaire. Shaun parked in the rocky layby and they walked down to the beach, the wind whistling around them. It was a beautiful cloudless day and the sea, calmer today, was a brilliant shade of aquamarine as the sun shone on it. He squeezed her hand tightly as they walked.

"Rebecca, I have not felt the way I feel about you for anyone, ever. I never had feelings like this for Renee. She wouldn't even visit Ireland, wasn't interested. Just wanted her party lifestyle and showy friends. In four days, you have stolen my heart. I want you to live here with me, in the house. We can build a new life together, just the two of us. I will love you, protect you, adore you. You never have to be afraid of anyone or anything again. Will you stay with me?" She looked up at him, and at that moment, she knew it was the right thing to do. Her destiny, their destiny. He kissed her, brushing away the tears that spilled down her cheeks.

"Don't cry, darling, it's time to be happy..."

They walked the length and breadth of the sands, as she cried, and they laughed, and talked.

"I love this place!" she called out at the top of her voice, as the wind whipped around them and the waves crashed on the sand.

6pm.

"James, it's Mum."

"Hey Mum, how's it going? You still at the spa?"

"I'm leaving your dad, James."

"What? Bloody hell, Mum! What's happened?"

"I will tell you when I see you, darling."

"Ok… where's Dad? At home? Should I call him?"

"It's up to you. I'll come and see you soon, darling."

"Ok Mum, look, it's ok, you know! He's a grumpy bastard, I don't know what's happened, but it's ok. We don't know how you've put up with him, all these years!"

A more difficult conversation followed with Sam. Angry at her, at first, then he got upset. She understood, she had expected it, he had always been the more sensitive of the two. Rebecca was due back at work the day after next, but she decided she would leave the call to the office until the next morning, she felt emotionally drained. She'd heard no more from Nigel. Of course, she would have to go to the house and get some things, but for now, she'd take each day as it came.

9pm.

They had talked for hours, just lying there, on the brass bed, arms wrapped around each other. They talked about the future, the past, their hopes and fears, dreams and desires. Rebecca felt exhausted, but at peace with her decision.

"It's late, shall we go get some dinner?" he suggested.

The beautiful day had turned into a spectacular night, the sky literally awash with stars, as they walked to the pub. The few locals that had been there the last time they visited nodded, winking at Rebecca. They ordered freshly caught sea-bass with new potatoes and fine green beans, and her favourite crisp Sauvignon. While they were eating, her phone buzzed in her bag and she saw it was Nigel. She turned it off.

"I'll come back to Richmond with you. You aren't going to the house by yourself." Shaun said, as they ate. "I have to go back to London, anyway." She nodded, grateful that she wouldn't have to go back there alone. After they had finished dinner, they strolled back to the cottage, arms wrapped around each other.

"I will have to call him." She whispered.

"I know, but you don't have to tonight, darling." He wrapped her in his arms so tightly she almost couldn't breathe.

"I love you." he murmured in her ear.

Shaun unlocked the door of the cottage and led her inside, gently pulling her to him as he kicked the door closed. He lowered his mouth to hers, and their lips and tongues locked in a passionate kiss as he gently eased her jacket off her shoulders.

His fingers slipped under her jumper, gently easing it over her head as he lowered his mouth to her breasts, sucking and licking her breasts. He picked her up and carried her to the bedroom, lying her down on the bed gently as he undressed her, then himself, looking into her eyes. Then, as he lowered himself onto her, he raised her arms above her head, holding them there with one hand as he eased himself into her slowly. They looked into each other's eyes, as he thrust deeper and deeper, climaxing together as she pulled him into her, her legs wrapped around him tightly.

Chapter 8.

Nigel.

"Dad? Dad, it's me, it's James!" He said.

Nigel dropped the phone. He retrieved it, stumbling into an armchair, breathless.

"Are you ok, Dad?"

"Your mother has left me..." he muttered, incoherently.

"Look, I know Dad. She called me and told me. I'm sorry, Dad. Dad? Dad, are you ok?"

Nigel had passed out.

Day 6.

Rebecca dialled the office just after nine. Lucy answered, sounding pleased when she heard Rebecca's voice.

"Hi Becs! How are you? We really miss you!"

"Hi Luce, I really need to talk to Jackie, I have to take some more leave," she said.

Lucy put her call through.

"Jackie, it's Rebecca. I need more time off, if it's possible? I've... well, I've left Nigel, and I have to arrange things..."

"Oh, I'm so sorry, Rebecca! What a tough time for you! Did the retreat make your mind up for you?"

"Yes, kind of." she replied.

Day 7.

After breakfast, they drove back out to the house again. While Shaun stood outside talking to the builders, she wandered slowly around the house, opening cupboards and doors and taking in the wonderful views from every angle.

She walked up the oak staircase, imagining going up to bed with him, waking up with him, living here, with him! While she stood in the front bedroom, gazing out at the sea, he came up quietly behind her and kissed her neck softly.

"This will be our room. We must get a bed, soon! Furniture! We have this place to fill, make homely..."

"Shaun, are you sure? Is this right? Us... me... leaving my home, my life behind? Am I dreaming?" she whispered, wretched tears falling from her eyes again. He pulled her to him and held her so tightly she thought she would faint. He kissed away her tears and stroked her hair, cupping her face as he looked at her.

"Like I told you, darling, I have never felt like this. I was quite happy to come back here, alone, live out here looking at that view every day. Work from here, with the occasional trip away when I need to. I wasn't looking for anyone, but when I first saw you at the airport, I felt drawn to you. I can't explain it, but now, look! We are together, in love with each other! If it is a dream, it's the only one I want to have!"

The cream envelope landed on the mat with a thud. Nigel picked it up, saw its black stamp, "*Down & Sons,*" and knew immediately what it contained. Throwing it on the side table, he grabbed his mobile, dialling the number quickly. It was answered almost immediately.

"I need to see you!" He said.

"Ok, give me half an hour."

Nigel hung up, glancing at himself in the mirror as he patted his hair down. He picked up the envelope, and, as he tore it open, he saw the words "*Petition for Divorce Proceedings*" at the top of the letter. Tossing it back down, he left the house, slamming the door as he usually did.

Hurrying, he made his way down the street, crossing at the lights and carrying on until he reached the now familiar path that led to the flat. Nigel approached the front door and put his key into the lock at the same time as Stuart opened it, pulling him inside in an embrace, as the door clicked shut behind them.

Day 8.

They landed at London City Airport and hired a car. Rebecca felt uneasy as they drove out, heading for Richmond. Everything had changed since she left here, and she didn't want to be back. Safe in the knowledge that Nigel would be at work, she planned to collect a few things from the house to tide her over, until the entire process had been dealt with. Jackie had allowed her another ten days off, during which she would hand her resignation in. She felt slightly guilty that she hadn't told her absolutely everything, but the next few days were the most important ones to deal with. Eventually, they would all know everything.

Shaun followed the sat nav, through the slow lunchtime traffic. As they drew near, he suggested lunch at a pub by the river. He pulled into "The Heron," one that Rebecca knew of, but hadn't been in before. It looked inviting enough, as they made their way in. It had been a really early start with a rushed breakfast and Rebecca, realising she was starving, could feel the beginnings of a dull headache.

They ordered drinks and sat at a table that overlooked the river.

"We should be quick, Shaun. I want to get in and out of there, as quickly as possible."

"I know, darling. Let's choose…" She decided all she could face was a Ploughman's, and he went up to the bar to place their order. As she watched him go, tall and broad shouldered, in his Donegal tweed jacket and navy Diesel jeans, she felt a familiar surge of desire, mingled with anxiety.

"It's that one, on the right. Number forty- five." Rebecca pointed, feeling nervous when she saw the house.

"How long do you think you need?" he asked.

"I'll be as quick as I can, maybe half an hour?"

He gently kissed her. "I'll be waiting."

Not bothered if any of their neighbours were watching, she let herself in, the wooden front door sticking as it always had. She gave it a shove and entered the house, glancing about quickly. There was stuff everywhere, washing hanging on the banister, shoes and socks discarded, piles of mail on the console. The house smelt musty, old. Making her way upstairs, she tried to think rationally.

In their bedroom, which she hadn't slept in since the boys were little, the bed lay unmade and the room smelt stale.

She opened the creaky wardrobe door to find her larger suitcase. As she pulled it out from the back of the cupboard, something caught on it. Another bag, a holdall of some sort, its zip half undone. Placing her suitcase on the floor, she reached for the holdall, looking inside it gingerly.

Amongst its contents, she saw underwear, but not anything that belonged to her. Horrible cheap nylon black and red knickers, stockings, a suspender belt, padded bras. Feeling sick, she looked further into the bag and saw make up: lipsticks, powders, false eyelashes. There was a pair of red stiletto heels that were so enormous she knew. This bag belonged to Nigel… the things in it were his. Horrified, she threw the bag back into the wardrobe, its contents falling out as she did so. She ran to the toilet and threw up.

    She had to get out of there. Frantically emptying everything from her drawers into the suitcase, she grabbed what she could from the wardrobe, and shoved the doors closed, sobbing as she did so. Quickly emptying the bathroom cabinet of her things, she ran into the boys' old room, where she'd been sleeping, and picked up the photos of them that had been on the bedside table. Making her way back downstairs, suitcase in hand, the tears were streaming down her face. She rummaged through the drawer in the office, grabbing a few of her bank cards and driving licence. Her laptop was the last thing, and as she let herself out, she looked back at the house. She felt strangely empty.

As she hurried back to the car, she was shaking violently. Shaun jumped out, took the suitcase off her and put it in the boot. He opened the passenger door and let her get in, hastily closing it after her. As they drove off, Rebecca could see her neighbour, Janine, looking out from her kitchen window, a strange expression on her face. Rebecca made a mental note to contact her, when this over. She had been kind over the years, and her boys had been friendly with James and Sam.

As she breathed in heavily, Shaun squeezed her hand. "You look pale, darling, and you're shaking!" he said, quietly.

"It's awful, worse than I could have imagined." She responded. He squeezed her hand, concern on his face.

"Let's get away from here."

As he opened the front door, he could smell Rebecca's scent lingering in the air. Nigel loved the smell of her... not that he'd ever told her. She had been here; he knew that as soon as he smelt her fragrance. Looking into the office, he saw her laptop had gone. Slowly walking upstairs, he wondered what time she had come here to get her things. Opening the wardrobe drawer, he knew her suitcase would not be there, and then he saw his own sordid secret lying there, exposed.

Nigel gave a huge, rasping cry, uncontrollably shaking as tears slopped down his face. He actually hated himself at that moment. He lay down on the bed, sobbing into the pillow. It was cruel, what he had put her through, he now realised. All to save his reputation at the stuffy firm he had given his working life to. To save the shame of what he was from his family, his friends. It had all been a lie, his entire life. The guilt weighed heavily on him.

When he was about fifteen, he'd started trying on his mother's lingerie whenever the opportunity arose. He realised it made him feel good, turned him on. Then he started using her make-up, always careful to put things back as he found them. Before long, he was doing it as often as he could, finding excuses to stay home whenever family outings occurred. He always felt ashamed afterwards, but that didn't stop him. He couldn't stop. After he'd left college and got his first job as an apprentice at the local insurance firm, his parents were so terribly proud. He knew that he would have to keep his secret hidden from everyone, so he set about looking for a girlfriend.

It was at the local dance hall when he first saw Rebecca, a shy looking petite young girl of 18. She looked so innocent, and as Nigel watched her shake her head at every offer of a dance, he thought he'd try his luck. He walked over slowly and stood next to her.

"Like a drink?" he asked.

She nodded, "lemonade, please."

As he came back with her drink, she smiled sweetly at him, a pinkish tinge to her cheeks.

"She'll do," he thought to himself, wryly.

Over the next few weeks, they went out on a few dates and got along fairly well. Nigel realised he'd found himself an easy cover up for his double life, which he carried on with, secretly.

He discovered she'd never had a boyfriend, which stood him in good stead for when sex eventually reared its' head... at least she would have nothing to compare him to. He introduced her to his poor, unsuspecting parents, who gave their instant approval, relieved Nigel was finally showing an interest in the opposite sex!

Six months later, they married in a Civil ceremony at the local Town Hall, a low-key affair with just a few close family and friends. They were living with his parents until they could afford a place, so they spent their wedding night in a small motel close by.

He had attempted to "make love" to her, but nothing happened. She had cried, he had said sorry, and then, as she slept, he crept into the cramped bathroom where her neatly folded wedding lingerie was placed on a stool. Nigel picked up the silky stockings, and tried to pull them on, snagging them as he did so.

He got hold of the silk French knickers, rubbing them against himself until they achieved the desired result. Then he climbed back into the small bed and forced himself on her, exploding into her with rage, without hearing her sobs of pain beneath him.

Chapter 9.

Day 9.

They had spent the night in a lovely little boutique hotel, right on the river. Its huge memory foam bed welcomed them as they fell into it, exhausted after the day's events. Over dinner, she told Shaun about her discovery at the house. He had held his head in his hands, shaking it with disbelief. His anger was evident, but she felt relief now, a certain calmness. It was all out in the open for her, at least. It explained alot about the relationship she had had with Nigel, but she would put the last 20 odd miserable years to the back of her mind, for now.

She awoke in Shaun's arms, feeling his arousal pressing into her. She felt herself pushing herself back into him, and as he entered her gently from behind, he whispered, "I love you so much, Rebecca." His hands crept round, holding her breasts and rolling her nipples between gentle fingers, as he moved faster in her. She reached down to pleasure herself, cupping him with her other hand. Gathering pace together, they climaxed to a shuddering halt. The sunlight filtered in gently through the venetian blinds, and they lay, entwined, for what seemed an eternity.

"We should get ready… it must be nearly 12?" she finally murmured.

"Yes, it is, darling." He kissed her shoulder, watching her as she rose from the bed.

They took a slow shower together, soaping each other under the powerful jets. As she dressed and applied quick makeup, he made coffee and looked at her, wantonly. She looked back at him, blushing at the look in his eyes.

James and Sam.

They were meeting the boys at a nearby pub for lunch. Rebecca was nervous. She had told them she would bring Shaun, having only explained briefly who he was, and how they had met. James had seemed fine about the meeting, but Sam less so. At 1.30, they sat in the pub garden, waiting. The September sun felt good on their faces as they held hands, and she told him more about the boys.

James and Sam arrived together, and Rebecca waved at them from their table. James smiled, hugging Rebecca.

'Hi Mum! You look great!"

Sam held back, uncertain. Rebecca held her hands out to him. "Hello darling."

"This is Shaun" said Rebecca, as he stood and held his hand out to each of the boys. James pumped his hand enthusiastically, while Sam held back, shifting nervously from one foot to another.

Eventually, he mumbled a "Hi" as Shaun went off to get the drinks.

"So, what's the story, Mum?" James asked.

As Rebecca told them about Shaun and their meeting, she chose her words carefully, so as not to betray Nigel. He was their Father, after all. Whether they thought he'd been much of one, she would never ask. James, the stronger of the boys, had always stood up to him, especially when he'd given Rebecca a hard time over something... or nothing. Sam, however, had been a timid, shy child, and hid away from confrontation. She looked at her dear boys and wished she'd left Nigel when they were little. She'd been so trapped. A baby bird in a not so gilded cage.

When Shaun returned with the drinks, the atmosphere was less tense, and as they chose from the menu, Rebecca felt more certain than ever that she was making the right decision.

"Ireland? Where?" James asked, surprised.

Shaun spoke. "I have built a house, it's in a rural part of Donegal, right near the sea. It's where I'm from, originally. Your Mother has fallen in love with it... we are going to be living there from around November time. You'll come and visit?"

"Well, yeah, sure, but what about Dad? Does he know?" asked Sam, his voice wavering.

"I have asked your Dad for a divorce, but he doesn't know I'm going to Ireland, yet."

The boys looked at each other, then back at the couple in front of them, so obviously in love and well suited to each other. "Well, you have my blessing Mum, I know Dad's been a difficult bloke to live with..." said James, and Sam nodded sadly, in agreement.

As they said their goodbyes, Rebecca held both boys tightly. "I'm not leaving you, boys. I'll always be there for you, you know that!"

"Yes, we know, Mum." they both said, in unison. They hugged Rebecca again, shook hands with Shaun and walked off to James' car, waving. Rebecca inhaled deeply, as Shaun squeezed her hand, tightly.

Day 10.

Shaun had to head up to the City for some meetings, and Rebecca had arranged to meet Nigel at a café in town, at 11am. As they kissed goodbye, Shaun hugged her tightly. "Don't take any shite from him" he whispered. She felt sick with nerves as she waited in the café. Nigel was late, it was nearly 11.15 when he finally showed up, looking equally nervous himself. They ordered their coffees, and while they waited for them, Nigel looked at her.

"I got the papers, Rebecca. I'm giving my consent to the divorce."

She looked at him, trying to rid her mind of what she had found in the wardrobe.

"Why are you not contesting it, Nigel?" she asked. This was actually not what she had expected at all.

He lowered his voice, looking down into his coffee. "Because I have been living a lie, for years. I was trying to make believe I could live with the deceit, lead a normal life, with you, then the boys. Because I am a coward.

I'm so sorry, Rebecca. I wish I had been honest with you from the beginning." He looked at her, his eyes welling with tears.

"Nigel, I found stuff, in the wardrobe. It was yours, right? Is that what you are talking about, living a lie?"

He nodded, and at that moment she felt overwhelming pity for him.

"I'm sorry." he said again.

"How long?" she asked.

"Since I was 15."

She felt a deafening silence crashing in her ears. "Why? Why did you ever marry me?"

"I told you, I was... I am... a coward! I couldn't have let anyone know! Then I got the apprenticeship... they'd have let me go if they found out!"

"So, it was all about you, Nigel." She choked, feeling bitterly angry.

"Rebecca, I'm sorry. I won't stand in your way. I'll give you half of everything. The boys will be financially secure, with their trust funds. Do... do they know anything?"

"Only that I'm leaving you, that's all."

He stood up, his chair scraping back on the tiled floor. "I'll sign the forms, today ..." he said, slowly walking away.

Day 11.

Dark Rain Organics.

"Come in, come in!" Jackie was pleased to see Rebecca. Alan sat, looking nervous, but then, he was of a nervous disposition. Rebecca sat down and took a deep breath.

"I'm leaving... England."

"What!" they both said, unanimously.

"I'm leaving Nigel, and I'm going to live in Ireland… with Shaun."

"Shaun?"

"Yes!" she wanted to shout at them, both sitting there with mouths wide open.

Jackie looked bemused, then stood and reached for Rebecca's hand.

 "My dear, I know you have been unhappy for such a long time. If you now have a chance to find happiness, then you have our blessing."

"Thank you, Jackie," Rebecca whispered, as her eyes welled with tears.

"When do you go? We could let you take the rest of your leave as notice?" Alan, ever practical, said. As Rebecca explained her next moves, they listened intently, nodding understandingly. Jackie spoke next. "Will you work, in Ireland? Only, we really don't want to lose you. Maybe you could sell Dark Rain over there for us, freelance? Open up the Irish market? What do you think?" Rebecca looked at them both, so dear and kind. "I will bear that in mind, thank you so much. I'll get settled, and I'll be in touch, I promise."

They got up, Alan hugged her awkwardly, while Jackie embraced her as a mother would a child. "Good luck, we hope everything works out for you!" As she left their office, the girls out front looked at her expectantly. "I'll explain all! Can we meet for drinks after you finish?" She suggested. Lucy and Mia nodded in unison... "usual place?" they both said.

Rebecca smiled, nodding. Craig's bar, they had enjoyed many fun nights there, over the years. "Is 6pm ok?" She suggested. "See you there!" They replied, giggling.

Day 12.

Rebecca stretched, feeling the length of Shaun against her. Her head felt slightly groggy. One drink the night before had turned into a few, as she had filled the girls in on her news. Shaun had come and collected her from "Craig's," and Lucy and Mia, giggling, had shaken hands with him. "Now we can see why our lovely Rebecca is leaving us!" Mia had said, the more outspoken of the two.

"She'll be in excellent hands." Shaun replied, winking at them as he'd pulled Rebecca into him. They'd said their goodbyes, and Shaun had given Rebecca a supporting arm as they walked along the quiet street, back to the hotel.

"What time do you want to go back to the house, darling?" He asked, as Rebecca groaned. It was the last thing she felt like doing. But go, she must. She had little to get, one more suitcase would do it. They left after breakfast, which they'd taken outside on the terrace, in the bright morning sunshine.

"I'll drop you there, and wait around the block, ok?"

"Thank you for your support... I would never have imagined I would be where I am, right now."

"Nor I," Shaun smiled, taking her hand in his. "But I wouldn't change a thing."

Back at the hotel that afternoon, Rebecca made the call to her parents in France.

"Hello darling! Where have you been? We've called a couple of times!"

"Hi, Mum. I went to a spa retreat... in Ireland, Buncragga, you know?"

"Really? Why there, of all places? There are some fabulous places here, you know! There's a Clarins spa down the road! Could have come and seen us?"

"I am coming to see you, Mum. And... is it ok if I bring... a friend?"

"Oh, who? What about the boys? We've not seen them for ages!"

"His name is Shaun. And the boys are back at Uni. Mum, I'm leaving Nigel. We are getting a divorce. Shaun is my new partner, and I'd really like you and Dad to meet him.

There was silence.

"Oh, my goodness! I don't know what your father will say! Are you sure? How long have you known this chap? Where did you meet? When are you thinking of coming?"

"Mum, I'll explain all when I see you. If it's a problem, we'll stay in a B&B."

"Goodness gracious! I wouldn't hear of it! I'll talk to your Dad. When did you say you're coming?"

"Well, is next week ok?"

She sighed as she ended the call. Lying back into the soft pillows, she felt exhausted, but relieved she'd made the call. Mind you, her mother had a knack for making her feel that way, talking nine to the dozen as she did. Shaun came and lay beside her, stroking her hair gently as she fell asleep. When she woke up, it was dusk, and she could just make Shaun out in the dim light. He was sitting in the chair by the bed, just watching her.

"Hello, darling. You've had a good couple of hours sleep, how do you feel?"

"Better. I need never go back there now. There's nothing more I want from there."

She sighed as she looked at the suitcase she had packed this morning. She'd taken the photo albums and school photos from the bureau, Nigel would not miss them, and some jewellery her Mother had given her. Her Waterford crystal wine glasses; a wedding present from Aunt Norah, her favourite coats, a couple of jumpers, the rest of her underwear, socks and boots.

That was all. All that she needed from the home that had become like a prison, full of belongings she realised she cared nothing for. Shaun got up from the chair and walked over to her. He took her in his arms, kissing her deeply.

"Shall I run you a nice bath? Then we could order room service?" She

breathed him in deeply and smiled.
"That would be lovely."

Chapter 10.

France.

They left the Eurotunnel, heading south out of Paris on the A10, towards Bordeaux.

"It's about a five hour drive, plenty of time for you to learn everything you need to know about my parents!" Rebecca laughed.

"Should I be worried?" Shaun asked, the pretence of a slight furrow on his brow.

"No... as soon as Mum hears your accent and finds out where you're from, she'll be convinced you know all her relatives, alive or not! You'll be accepted into the fold immediately, I promise!"

She settled into the soft leather seat of the convertible sports car Shaun had insisted on hiring. It was so humid; she was glad she'd worn her Zara button through linen shirt dress. She'd tied her hair back in a low ponytail, and as they sped off, she was grateful for the breeze the convertible roof allowed. As they drove, she told Shaun about her Aunt Norah, her Mum's sister, whose house in Donegal they'd spent summer holidays at when she and her sister were kids. How her Mother would haggle outrageously with the local fishermen over prices for their catch, as they walked past Norah's cottage after a day's fishing.

She flirted with them, too, having grown up with most of them. She remembered how Dad would be so embarrassed, and Norah would tell her off. How different her Mum and Norah were. And how she and her sister would be out on the beach all day, rock-pooling, swimming, exploring. She told him what an idyllic childhood they had had.

"So, your parents are Kathleen and Robert?"

"Yes, but they'll ask you to call them Kath and Bob. Dad's really easy-going, but Mum will bombard you!"

They sped through the beautiful countryside, towards Nantes, where they planned to stop for lunch. The sun beat down on them as they listened to a random French radio station that played songs they could sing along to... Dire Straits, ELO, Guns n' Roses, Elton John and some they couldn't, but loved all the same... Edith Piaf, Julio Iglesias and Charles Aznavour. They realised they had the same taste in music and laughed intermittently at each other when one of them got the words wrong!

Three and a half hours later, they arrived in Nantes, and parked up to find somewhere to have lunch. As they walked along by the river Loire, hand in hand, Rebecca thought how it she felt like she'd been with Shaun for ever. It felt so comfortable, so natural. They eventually found a small café on the riverbank, serving a fresh seafood "plat du jour" for 15 euros. It looked inviting, so they took their seats at a little bistro table overlooking the river. The waiter brought carafes of rose' and water, and Rebecca ordered the platter for them, in her basic French.

"I'd love to explore here, there's so much to see!" she commented. "Yes, there is. We can come back sometime?" he said, taking her hand and stroking her delicate fingers. He reached his lips to her hand, kissing it gently. She blushed, and sipped the chilled rose', as she sighed with pleasure.

They got back on the road after lunch, heading towards les Landes, the pine forest region covering a vast area, south-west of Bordeaux, another two hours drive. As Shaun drove expertly through the beautiful countryside, she could feel her eyes closing… she felt sleepy, probably from the wine. Shaun looked across at her as she slept, noticing the fine beads of perspiration on her upper lip, and the gentle trickle of sweat running down between her breasts. Eventually, he slowed down, turning off the main road down a track that was signposted "Landes de Gascogne." Rebecca jolted awake, "Gosh, sorry! How long have I been asleep? You must be tired of driving! Shall I take over?" He looked over at her. "It's fine, darling. I was going to stop for a bit… have a look at the forest…"

Before long, an ocean of greenery lay before them, thousands of Bordeaux pine trees undulating as far as the eye could see. The road through the trees was hazy, a cloudy mix of sawdust, bark and pine needles, with lay-bys full of enormous felled trunks.

"This is breath-taking!" Rebecca gasped. "I've never seen it! Nigel would never stray from the major roads, when we used to drive here, not that he came with us that many times..."

"I've always wanted to see it." Shaun said, as he parked in a small clearing hidden by pine trees. "And I wanted to do this..."

He turned the car off and leaned across to her, his tongue gently tasting the sweat above her lip. She felt the familiar burning sensation in her groin as she opened her mouth to taste his, murmuring his name. He unbuttoned the first few buttons of her dress, kissing the trickle of moisture that led down between her breasts. She groaned as he said, "Come here, sit astride me." She looked around, nervously. "But..."

"It's fine, it's siesta time here, and it's Saturday! There's no one around."

Without hesitation, she nimbly lifted herself over the gear stick, and as he unbuttoned his jeans, she pulled her panties down and lifted herself onto him. He was as hard as she was wet, and as she ground herself onto him they came quickly, desperately, her hands raking through his thick hair, as she closed her eyes and buried her face into his neck. The scent of pine was heady, spicy, as they breathed heavily into each other. The sound of grasshoppers surrounded them, as she gently lifted herself off him and fell back into her seat, laughing. "Shaun, you are a wicked man!" He smiled at her, his eyes flashing sexily. "You bring it out in me!" He kissed her and started the car.

They stopped at Arcachon Bay, where swimmers and surfers bobbed about on the white waves, the sea an azure blue. Here, they could see the beginning of Europe's largest dune, the "Dune Du Pilat" which stretched ahead of them for 3 kilometers.

"Mum and Dad like to come here, for the oysters!" Rebecca said.

"It's lovely, something about it reminds me of home, the dunes and endless white sand, I'm guessing...it wouldn't be the weather!" Shaun commented.

They walked around the pretty town for a bit, before setting off on the last leg of their journey to Biscarosse. As they drove on through the beautiful countryside, Shaun told her about his parents.

"Eileen was my Mam, she and my Dad, Seamus, were married 55 years. I'm the oldest, at 44, then there's Joe, Fergal and Bridget. Joe and Fergal are in the USA, and Bridget, well you'll meet her. She's still in our village. I've not seen my brothers for a few years, but they are planning a trip over to Ireland to see the family and the new house, probably in the Spring, so you'll get to meet them then."

"Oh right, I shall look forward to that. I'll need to visit my sister, Andrea, and her family... perhaps before we... go back to Ireland?" It sounded strange, and unreal, when she said that, but he looked across at her, and squeezing her hand, said "Yes, we'll do that."

As dusk fell, they arrived at 'Villa Clemency.' The sky was a calming shade of lavender. They drove through lemon groves, laden with their harvest, and pulled up outside the open front door, its terracotta tiled porch offering a cool welcome.

"Hello darling!" her Mother's voice rang out shrilly. "Bob, they are here!"

Rebecca hugged her Mum as Shaun got their bags out of the boot. "Let me look at you! It's been too long!" Kath took Rebecca's hands, smiling.

"Mum, this is Shaun."

"Pleased to meet you, Kathleen."

"Oh, you must call me Kath, and here's Bob!"

Rebecca hugged her Dad and stood aside as he pumped Shaun's hand energetically.

"Come on in, we have cocktails ready!" Kath said excitedly, as Shaun and Rebecca followed them in.

They sat out on the veranda with their drinks, the sun slowly sinking on the horizon until hidden from view behind a forest of pine trees. Kath lit the lanterns that surrounded the seating area, as Bob refreshed their cocktails. "We've got slow-cooked bbq lamb for dinner!" he said, proudly.

"Lovely Dad, thank you... my favourite."

Kath came and sat back down, scrutinising Rebecca and Shaun.

"So, how did you two meet?" Kath asked.

Shaun reached for Rebecca's hand, and, smiling, said, "We were destined."

"Oh, my goodness! How romantic! Tell us more!" Kath exclaimed.

Bob cleared his throat and stood up. "I'll check the lamb!"

"Oh, don't mind him!" she said, once he was out of earshot. "He finds romance embarrassing!"

"Well, Kath, I think you live in a fairly romantic place!" Shaun said, laughing.

The atmosphere was jovial, and Rebecca felt relaxed. She'd known they would accept Shaun easily.

"Now, I've put you in the guest annexe, more... private for you. You'll probably want to freshen up before dinner, shall we say about an hour? Dad's already put your things in there for you."

"Thanks, Mum. I hope we haven't put you out?"

"Don't be daft... it's wonderful to have you here!"

Rebecca led Shaun round the back of the villa where the annexe was all lit up, ready for them. She opened the heavy wooden door and stood aside to let Shaun in. Bob had lit the fire in the lounge area, and the terracotta floor tiles felt warm underfoot.

The small kitchenette had a basket of fresh fruit and bread on the countertop, and there was milk and butter in the pantry, Rebecca noticed.

Shaun came up behind her, reaching his arms around her waist and bending to kiss her neck. She turned around, kissing him hard on the lips, as he responded, probing her lips open with his tongue.

"God, I want you, darling" he whispered. "Later…" she murmured, her eyes half closed. Taking his hand, she showed him the large bedroom with its French carved four-poster bed, and en-suite shower. White fluffy towels and robes were placed on the towel rack, and L'Occitane soap, shower gel, and body lotion sat beside the sink.

"This is superb!" he said, eyeing the bed up suggestively.

"I've never even slept in that bed! This is normally for paying guests! But Mum knows great hospitality, and she has fantastic taste." Rebecca said, smiling.

   Shaun showered as she unpacked, and, looking at the bed, she turned the covers down in preparation. The crisp white bedlinen looked inviting. She shivered with pleasure, anticipating being between those sheets with him, tonight.

He came out of the shower, a towel around his waist, droplets of water clinging to the dark hair on his chest. As he casually pulled the towel off and got dressed, she looked on brazenly. Catching her eye, he winked. "All yours later, darling!" She blushed and sauntered to the shower, undressing as she went, whilst he let out a slow, sexy wolf whistle.

They made their way out to the veranda where Kath had laid the dining table with white linen, crystal glasses, candles and lavender sprigs at each placemat. There were baskets of fresh bread, bowls of salads and new potatoes. Bob was carving the lamb at the end of the table.

"Oh Mum, it looks beautiful!" said Rebecca, as Shaun let out a quiet "Wow! Amazing!"

"Oh, thank you! We've not had guests for ages, and I especially love to spoil family!" she said, looking at Shaun pointedly.

"Do sit down, would you like red or white wine?" Bob asked.

They both chose red, which he poured from a crystal carafe for them. As they sat down to eat, the Gipsy Kings played from the outdoor speakers, the crickets just audible above the music. The setting couldn't have been more perfect.

"This lamb is fantastic." Shaun complemented Bob.

"Ah, a secret recipe, perfected many years ago!"

At which Kath told them exactly how to prepare the lamb, listing all Bob's secret ingredients, as Shaun listened, and smiled. He looked across at Rebecca, thinking how beautiful she looked by candlelight, her eyes luminous and her skin glowing. Noticing how much she resembled her mother, but with her dad's dark colouring, he felt his heart swell with passion for her. Kath saw how he was looking at Rebecca and felt a well of emotion build up in her chest, as she quickly dabbed the corners of her eyes with a napkin.

"Mum, I'll help clear" Rebecca stood up and gathered the plates.

"It's alright! It won't take a minute. You sit and have a brandy with Dad, he's lighting the fire pit."

"I'll help." Shaun stood up, taking the plates from Rebecca. He followed Kath into the house. In the kitchen, she turned to look at him. "I've never seen her so happy, it's lovely for us. I won't be disrespectful about Nigel, but... well, let's just say, we never understood why she married him, let alone stayed with him, all these years!"

"Kath, we've fallen for each other, truly, madly, deeply! It might sound clichéd, but it's true. She's everything I've ever wanted in a woman, and I will cherish her forever."

Kath, feeling emotional again, smiled softly. "I love clichés!" she said.

They sat around the fire pit for a while, watching the flames cackle and hiss, until Rebecca realised how exhausted she was. She reached her hand to Shaun's knee. "Are you tired, after all that driving?"

"Yes, I think it's time for bed, darling."

They thanked Kath and Bob for the evening and strolled, hand in hand, back to the annexe. Watching them go, Kath said, "Well, I think our daughter is well and truly in love, dear."

"Yes, I think you're right, and I'd say I'm rather pleased with her choice. I like the fellow, much more convivial than

Nigel. Never got much out of him." Bob said.

"We'll find out more tomorrow, are you coming in now?" Kath asked, as she patted his knee lovingly.

The morning sun shone through the slats in the shutters, and Rebecca stretched, feeling the length of Shaun's lean, naked body. Realising she was naked, too, she thought back to the night before. She remembered him taking her nightdress off, and then kissing her entire body from head to toe, slowly and sexily, gently bringing her to a climax before he'd thrust deep into her, as she'd arched her back lifting her hips up to him.

They had fallen asleep, naked, entwined. Smiling to herself, she stretched out, languidly. Shaun made tea while she went to have a shower, bringing it to her and looking at her as she lathered herself with the verbena scented shower gel.

"They're great, your folks."

"I know, they really are... I wish they'd been around when... well, you know."

"Yeah, I know, darling."

He put the tea down, and, slipping off his boxers, stepped into the shower with her.

"I can do that..." he said, as he soaped her breasts, her buttocks and in between her legs. She moaned softly as he bent his head and sucked her nipples gently, feeling his arousal against her thigh. He lifted her up onto him, grasping her bottom and slowly pulsing into her as she gripped him with her thighs. "God, you are so damn sexy!" he groaned.

The water flowed over them as they shuddered into each other, backed up into the wall of the shower.

After, he gently dried her hair as she watched him in the mirror. "Wonder if anyone's done that in the parents' shower before?" she smirked. He smiled. "Well, if they haven't, I'm sorry for them. More tea, darling?"

"Good morning! How are we?" Kath asked, as she poured coffee from a large cafetiere.

"Morning, Mum" said Rebecca, as Shaun leant in to give her Mum a kiss on the cheek. "Thank you for making us so comfortable, Kath." He said. Kath smiled, and they sat down outside, drinking the coffee she had poured them. The view that lay before them, tall pine trees beyond which the sea was just visible, was beautiful. A hazy sun shone in the milky blue sky, before long it would be a dazzling blue as the sun burned through the haze.

"So, you met in Ireland?" Kath began.

"Well, on the way to Ireland… at the airport, actually." Said Rebecca.

"Oh!" Kath, for once, didn't know what to say.

Shaun took over as Bob came and joined them for coffee.

"I'm moving back to Donegal… I'm from a small village near Ardara. I was on the same flight as Rebecca, and, because of terrible weather, the plane had to abort landing into Kilmarnock. They diverted the aircraft to a tiny airport in the middle of nowhere, and then I offered Rebecca a lift to Buncragga."

"Oh, that was kind of you." said Kath.

Rebecca giggled. "Oh Mum, Shaun was brilliant. I was so scared on the flight.

He drove me to the spa at Buncragga so I didn't have to get the bus they had arranged for us.

Over the few days I was there, we met up and... well... I've decided to leave Nigel, as I told you on the phone."

Bob cleared his throat. "Shaun, do you play golf?" he asked.

"I do, yes. I'm a keen golfer, Bob."

"Would you like to join me for 9 holes this afternoon? The golf club isn't far. We can leave the ladies to chat?"

Golf arranged, Rebecca went with Kath to prepare lunch, collecting the bag of goodies she'd brought from England for them on her way.

"Oh! PG Tips... I'm nearly out! And Rich Tea... your Dad will be pleased!" Kath emptied the remaining contents of the bag onto the kitchen counter... there was Marmite, Dairy Milk bars, Pukka sleep tea, crumpets, teacakes, all the things Rebecca knew they missed from the UK.

"Bless you, darling, thank you. Now, lunch… how about a platter of ham, cheese, vine leaves, etcetera? Nice and easy? Then we could have a walk into town while they are golfing, if you like. I just need a few bits from the market."

"That sounds great, Mum."

After lunch, they strolled into the little town, stopping at a café in the main square beside an ornate stone fountain. Its spouting water droplets sparkled prettily in the sun. In fluent French, Kath ordered tea and cannelles for them; traditional caramelised cupcakes. Slowly and steadily, with deep, even breaths, Rebecca told her about Nigel.

"Oh, my God! I cannot believe it! You poor darling… what a ghastly discovery! Do the boys know anything?" Kath was horrified.

"No. I won't tell them. It's not fair. But I feel so angry, Mum! I've wasted my life living with an excuse of a man, in a dysfunctional marriage! How cruel of him, to live a lie! Make all of us live his lies!"

Tears welled up in Rebecca's eyes, as her Mum pulled her towards her chest and hugged her.

"It's not been a waste, you have the boys, and lovely young men they are, thanks to you. You are still young, and look what you have found, in Shaun! We very much approve, he is charming! But do you feel going to live with him so soon is the right thing? It will be an extraordinary existence there, you know! God knows, it didn't suit me, I couldn't wait to get away, as you know!"

"Yes, I know it's the right thing." Rebecca sobbed. "I've had the most amazing time with him in the few days I've known him, he is so kind and loving. We are meant to be together, Mum. And you know I've always loved Ireland, I'll know I'll be happy there.

It's not too far away from anyone, either, the nearest airport is only an hour and a half's drive... The house itself is fabulous, too. I must get Shaun to show you photos. It looks out to the Atlantic on one side, and the mountains at the back. The design... Shaun's design, it's out of this world!" Kath smiled softly as tears brimmed in her eyes.

"Then, you have our blessing. And I'm so sorry for all the hurt you've been through. Your Dad and I are always at the end of the phone whenever you need us."

"Thanks, Mum, I know." They drank their tea as the fountain tinkled beside them.

When they got back to the villa, Shaun and Bob had returned from golf, and were sitting on the sun loungers by the swimming pool. The afternoon sun was intense, and Rebecca thought how inviting the water looked. Shaun waved, beckoning to them.

"Come and join us! It's refreshing..." Rebecca looked at him, tanned and lean in his new Ted Baker turquoise shorts, a beer in his hand. "You look like you've been here a month!" she laughed. "You go on in, dear, I'll take the shopping in and come out soon." said Kath.

Rebecca went and changed, glad that they'd purchased swimwear for the trip. She unwrapped the Ted Baker bikini from its tissue paper, the bright floral print reminding her why she'd fallen in love with it when she saw it. As she undressed and put it on, she checked herself out in the cheval mirror. The bra top fitted perfectly and gave her breasts a subtle lift. The high-waisted briefs were adjustable at the sides, so she pulled the strings to make them slightly briefer. "Not bad," she thought to herself, as she tied the matching sarong round her waist, and went out to the pool. Shaun looked at her admiringly, as she undid the sarong and sat at the edge of the pool, the cool water lapping her ankles.

"How was golf?" she asked.

"He's pretty good, is Shaun! A better handicap than I!" her Dad said, smiling.

"Nice course, Bob. And of course, better playing in weather like this. When you come visit us in Ireland, I'll take you out at Port Noo… but you'll need waterproofs!"

"Well, sometimes a bit of rain is a welcome sight. I quite miss it,

at times! Rebecca, a beer, darling?"

Bob got up to fetch her one, as Shaun slipped into the pool and rested his chin on her thighs.

"Coming in?" as he gently lifted her into the pool. She put her legs around his waist and kissed his shoulder.

"You look sensational in that costume." He said as he squeezed her bottom, pulling her into him.

Bob came back with beers for them all, and they stood in the pool, chatting. The sun, high in the sky, shone down relentlessly.

After a couple of hours by the pool, they went back to the villa to get ready for dinner. Tonight, they were taking her parents out to a local seafood restaurant in the village. Shaun pulled her towards him as he reached around and undid her wet bikini top. She shivered as he rolled the briefs down over her hips and kissed her, his tongue prising her lips open. "You're all wet," he whispered.

She wore her All-Saints floral silk wrap dress, with her black gladiators, and fixed her still damp hair into a low, messy bun, a few loose tendrils framing her face. Silver hoops in her ears completed the outfit. Shaun whistled appreciatively when he saw her.

"You wear things well, gorgeous!"

"Thank you... you look pretty damn fine yourself."

He'd changed into black linen trousers and a white shirt, worn loose over the trousers, with tan leather sandals. Rebecca's parents were waiting for them on the terrace, and Bob handed them chilled flutes of prosecco as they approached.

"You two make such an attractive couple." Kath remarked, smiling at them.

"As do you and Bob!" Shaun replied.

"Flattery will get you everywhere, at our age!" Kath laughed, sliding her arm around Bob's waist.

Drinks finished, they set off for the village. It was dusk, and fireflies were appearing, like miniature torches lighting the way for them. Rebecca had reserved a table for them at the "O'Zinc" restaurant, a charming little place that she and her parents had dined at many times. The waiter seated them at an outdoor table, looking out on to "Place Charles de Gaulle." Candles were alight in elegant glass torch holders, dotted about the terrace. There were a few other diners, and a solitary musician strumming his guitar in the corner, the sound melodious in the tranquil setting.

The waiter brought carafes of white and red wine to the table, with a jug of sparkling water. Bob poured the wine, and they sat back to read the menus. They decided on sharing platters of seafood, meats and cheeses, along with olives, bruschettas and salads. Rebecca wanted Shaun to feel at ease, although she knew her parents had already accepted him as her "new" partner, and he seemed happy and relaxed in their company. She looked across at him, smiling, as he took her hand and winked at her.

"So, what are you two up to tomorrow?" Kath asked. "Have you seen much of this part of France, Shaun?"

"I have not, but I'm keen to. We stopped to look at the forest at Les Landes… and then when we got to Arcachon." he replied, looking at Rebecca as she blushed in the candlelight.

"Ah, well, there's a lot to do here in Biscarosse. There's the 14th century Montbran Castle, where you can see three lakes joined by a canal, Lakes Biscarosse, Cazaux and Sanguinet, only about 7kms from the town. And the fortified church of St. Martin... if you like churches... it's built of local stone called 'Garluche,' three naves built with pink bricks, white stone vaulted ceilings, beautiful stained glass and unique woodwork... it's quite something." Bob told them, and went on "and near the church, there's a huge elm tree that carries a famous legend... in 1450 a young shepherdess, Adeline, found guilty of being unfaithful to her fiancé, was forced to be exposed, naked, under the 'Tree of Justice' for one day. By sunset, she had died of shame and sorrow. The next day, exactly where she had laid her head, flowers bloomed, looking like a bride's white bouquet. Since then, every year in May, white flowers bloom in exactly the same spot!"

"We shall have to come back in May, see if it's true!" Shaun said, squeezing Rebecca's hand.

"Well, perhaps a day's sightseeing tomorrow then, Shaun?" Rebecca responded, squeezing his hand back.

Dinner finished, they strolled back to 'Villa Clemency. ' The night air was cool, and the sky was awash with stars.

"Night cap, anyone?" Bob asked, hopefully.

"Cheers Bob, that'd be grand." Shaun replied. Rebecca and her Mum went inside to make Irish coffees, and then they all sat out on the terrace, around the flickering firepit, until well past midnight.

The next day was spent sightseeing, and though Rebecca had visited both castle and church before, it felt as though she was seeing them for the first time, with renewed interest and... hope? She couldn't quite put her finger on it, but she knew she'd never felt like it before.

After looking at the beautiful church of St. Martin, they wandered up the cobbled street until they came to "The Tree of Justice" that Bob had told them about.

Standing under its branches, hidden from view, Shaun pulled her towards him and kissed her gently. She melted into his powerful arms, kissing him back forcefully. Cupping her face with his hands, he gazed into her eyes. "Marry me, Rebecca." She gasped, sobbing. "Oh my God! Yes, yes, I will, Shaun!" He rubbed his thumb along her bottom lip. "I love you so much darling, I will cherish you as my wife, forever." They strolled back to the villa hand in hand, euphoric about their decision. The sun, low in the sky now, gave the clouds a dusky pink glow.

"Mum, Dad, we have something to tell you." Rebecca said, almost bursting with excitement. Bob looked up at them, over his glasses. Kath put her book down, a twinkle in her eyes.

"Kath, Bob, I have asked Rebecca to become my wife. I hope this meets with your approval?"

"Wonderful news! Of course it does! Doesn't it, Bob?" Kath jumped up and hugged Rebecca, then Shaun. Bob stood up, and, shaking Shaun's hand, nodded his approval.

"We need champagne, Bob!" Kath nudged him.

"I shall get some immediately, give me half an hour to pop to town!"

"Thank you, Dad! We'll go get changed and see you soon." Said Rebecca, as she grabbed Shaun's hand. "Thanks, Mum. We'll be back in a while." Kath hugged herself as she watched them walk away.

They let themselves back into the annexe, and Rebecca turned to Shaun, smiling.

"Well, you are full of surprises!"

He looked serious. "I don't want to waste another minute of my life, without you," he said, pulling her to him and kissing her with fervour.

They showered and changed, he into his black linen trousers with a paisley Boss shirt. Rebecca chose the only evening dress she had, pleased she'd brought it with her. It was a black silky halter neck with a low back, the skirt split to her thigh. She'd bought it from one of her favourite shops, Massimo Dutti, for a work Christmas party. Nigel had criticised her when he saw her in it, she remembered. "You look sluttish in that." he'd said, cuttingly. But she had worn it anyway, and everyone at the party had said how lovely she looked in it.

Banishing him from her mind, she slid the dress on, trying to fasten the button at the back of her neck. Shaun let out a low whistle, as he said, "here, let me do that." He gently secured the single button and turned her toward him. "Stunning, simply stunning, darling."

She blushed, and he smiled at that. "You are going to make one gorgeous bride."

Bob was waiting on the terrace, fiddling with matches and trying to light candles. "Blasted things, must be damp!" He muttered to himself.

"Here you are, and how lovely you look! I have booked a table at "La Caravelle" ... our treat, to congratulate you both! But champagne, first!" Kath pulled the bottle of Dom Perignon that Bob had returned with from the ice bucket. Bob had finally managed to light the candles, and taking the champagne from Kath, he popped the cork, filling the chilled flutes she'd put out on a silver tray. Shaun and Rebecca took one each, and Kath and Bob clinked glasses with them.

"To the happy couple!" Bob said, at which Kath started crying.

"Mum, stop! You'll start me off!" Rebecca felt tears welling in her eyes.

"La Caravelle" was located in a prime position in the town, opposite Lake Biscarosse. The maitre d' led them to a table on the terrace, overlooking the lake, which was shimmering in the moonlight.

"Champagne, s'il vous plaît!" Kath said, as she sat down. The waiter poured champagne and handed them red leather- bound menus.

"The steak is very good here, Shaun. They do it over an open grill." Bob commented.

They all ordered grilled tiger prawns to begin, then Shaun and Bob had the steak, medium rare, and Rebecca and her Mum chose the fresh fish special, grilled "sole meuniere," which was boned and plated by their waiter, at the table.

"Delicious!" Rebecca said, as she tasted the perfectly cooked sole, served with new potatoes, fresh lemon, and parsley.

The steaks arrived, sizzling on stone platters, with baskets of frites to accompany them.

As they ate, an over excited Kath wanted to know when they thought they might get married, and where.

"We haven't talked about that yet, Mum!" Rebecca exclaimed.

"Oh, I'm sorry, darling. I know it's only just happened... but it's so thrilling! When will you tell the boys?"

"Not yet and please, mention nothing Mum! I... we... need to get everything settled, then once we're in the house, we can start thinking ahead."

Shaun agreed, taking her hand and squeezing it reassuringly.

"You two will be the first to know of our plans," he chuckled.

"Are you okay?" Shaun asked, as they lay in bed that night, their last at the villa.

As Rebecca snuggled into him, she whispered, "Yes... I couldn't be happier, but I think my new fiancé should make love to me?"

He kissed her gently, his tongue probing her lips apart, as she opened her mouth to him. He slipped her nightdress from her shoulders, moving his lips to her breasts, sucking and biting her nipples as she felt his hardness grow against her. She pushed him back into the bed as she climbed astride him, guiding him into her deeply, as she arched her back and ground herself against him until they came together, in an explosive surge.

"God, I love you so much!" He cried out as he lifted her off himself and pulled her into him, tightly.

"I love you too, Shaun." She whispered, kissing him and laying her head on his chest, as they fell asleep like that.

"It's been lovely having you here, darling!" Kath hugged Rebecca as though she couldn't bear to let her go. "And Shaun! We both really like him, he seems to make you so happy, and that makes us happy."

"Thanks, Mum. We've so enjoyed being here. An unexpected holiday! I'll let you know when we're in the new house safely."

Shaun joined them and shook Bob's hand. Kissing Kath on each cheek, he said, "Thank you for such a grand welcome! You must come and see us in the new house."

"We will, we will." Bob nodded as he hugged Rebecca tightly.

They set off for Paris, Rebecca waving goodbye until her parents, and 'Villa Clemency' were out of sight.

Chapter 11.

Paris.

It was dusk when they arrived in Paris. Shaun had surprised Rebecca on the journey, telling her he had booked a night's accommodation at the "Hotel La Villa Saint Germain," a few minutes from the Seine. He revealed he'd done a bit of research and found its great location at the crossroads of three of Paris' most charming quarters. The Latin quarter, with its art galleries, the 7th century arrondissement and its antique dealers, and Opera with its luxury boutiques, stretching all the way to the Place Vendome. It was also near the Louvre, the Palais Royal and the Tuileries Garden, and Notre Dame Cathedral.

"When did you do your homework?" she asked, amazed.

"Well, I talked to your Dad about it after golf... actually, he was most helpful, said as far as he knew, you'd never stayed in Paris. I was going to ask you to marry me when we were here, but I couldn't wait another minute! That day in Biscarosse, under that tree... the time just seemed right."

Rebecca smiled at him and sighed happily. She had always wanted to see Paris, stay a few days, and it seemed fitting that her first time doing so should be with the man who had become the love of her life! Shaun parked up near to the hotel. It was a balmy evening, and the streetlights were just beginning to illuminate.

He got their bags from the boot, and they crossed over the street to the hotel. The doorman held open the glass front door for them as they walked into the lobby with its high ceiling, a centrally located sweeping staircase, marble floors, and mahogany wood panelling on the walls.

The concierge welcomed them warmly and checked them in to a room which had a lovely view of the Seine, as requested. Shaun winked at Rebecca, and the porter escorted them to their room. It was large, with classic, neutral décor giving it a modern, minimalist feeling. Rebecca crossed the room to look out of the floor to ceiling window, gasping when she saw the view. It was truly magical, the sky now a pinkish gold above the river, dark and mysterious, the city lights reflected on its surface. In the distance, she could see the Eiffel Tower, covered in golden lights, hundreds of them outlining the metal structure, topped by a huge beacon.

"Beautiful, look, Shaun!" as she took his hand and pulled him to her. "Did you know, those lights sparkle every hour, on the hour?" she said.

"I do, and I also know it's best seen from the river, as are most of the other famous landmarks, so I thought we might do a cruise before dinner?"

"I'd love that! I'll have a shower and change, though."

"Ok, darling. I'll phone down and ask the concierge to book it for 8pm? I read they sail hourly until 10pm."

The boat meandered slowly along the river, the sky now dark, but with a golden hue from all the city lights. They sat on narrow wooden benches next to the windows, and marvelled as they sailed past the Notre Dame, with its flying buttress structure and its 93 metre spire through the middle. Strategic lighting gave views of the dozens of chimeras and gargoyles lining its roof.

Shaun told Rebecca about when he was studying Architecture and spent three months in the city. He had, he said, gained so much inspiration from its wonderful buildings. He pointed out the Notre Dame's twin towers, once home to the famous hunchback, Quasimodo, and they could clearly see its equally famous bells.

The boat sailed on, past the Louvre, with its stunning pyramid design entrance, its position amongst classically designed buildings a stroke of architectural genius, merging old with new.
"I'd love to visit it… maybe tomorrow? I have always wanted to see the 'Mona Lisa' and 'Venus de Milo!'"

"We can, why not? We can do whatever you want. After all, we don't have to rush back to London, do we? I have the keys to the Islington flat until the end of the month. Why don't we stay tomorrow night, as well? I'm sure the room will be free for another night, as it's the end of the season. What do you think?" Shaun asked.

"Oh, can we? I'm free to do what I want, now... well, almost. I'd love to see more of the city tomorrow... with you as my tour guide!"

"Well, it was a long time ago I was here, but I'm sure we'll find our way around!" he laughed, placing his arm around her shoulders.

The cruise continued, as the host talked them through the sights, the next being the ornamental "Tuileries" gardens, designed by Queen Catherine de Medici in 1560, which they decided they would visit the next day. They could just make out its long lines of trees, and geometric design, in the dusk. At the next bend in the river, the "Grand Palais" and "Petit Palais" were visible, with their grand glass roofs and fabulous facades.

"These two buildings combine classical architecture with Art Nouveau, my favourite design period." Shaun told her as the boat passed under the Pont Alexandre 111, a bridge considered one of Paris' finest. Here, through the magnificent glass domes of the palaces, they could see their Art Nouveau lights, golden-winged horses, and cherubs adorning the ceilings… "Oh, my goodness! It's breath-taking!" Rebecca said breathlessly, wide eyed with amazement.

The cruise came to an end, and they stepped off the boat into the street, crowded now with evening revellers.

"Shall we walk back towards the hotel, find somewhere for dinner on the way?" Shaun suggested.

Rebecca nodded. It was late, and she realised how hungry she was. They found a cosy, typically Parisian restaurant, down a dimly lit side street. The setting was intimate and quiet, and they sat at a table near the window. Shaun ordered wine for them, and they both chose the fresh seafood pasta which, with clams, mussels, prawns and squid, sounded delicious.

"I so enjoyed the cruise. I'd never imagined you'd see such amazing views of the buildings!" Rebecca said. "It must have been so inspiring, studying here?"

"It was, I truly loved it. French didn't come easily to me, but I got by!"

Shaun told her about the room he'd rented in the Latin quarter, how it was freezing cold and rundown, but he hadn't minded then, as it was cheap.

"And I was young! My tastes have become very much more discerning, as I've got older!"

"Apparently!" she laughed.

Back at the hotel, Shaun opened the door to their room and let Rebecca in first. She kicked off her Converse, and went to lie down on the king-size bed, her head resting on the huge, soft pillows. "I'm so tired! And you must be... all that driving!" He looked across the room at her, as he undid the buttons on his shirt and tossed it on the nearby chair.

"Oh, I don't know... not that tired..." his eyes glinted, mischievously. He came and sat beside her, on the bed, and removing her socks, he massaged her feet with firm fingers.

"That feels good," she sighed.

He kissed her toes, and feet, and moved up the bed to lie beside her, one hand turning her face toward his, as he lowered his lips onto hers. She responded fervently, as his hands moved under her sweater, lifting it up over her head as his lips moved to her breasts, kissing and sucking each nipple through the soft satin of her bra, as she writhed and moaned beneath him.

"Let me undress you completely" he said, as he stood and unbuckled his belt, then unbuttoned his jeans, and pulled them off. He unzipped her jeans, dragging them off her as she lifted her hips. Then he slipped his fingers into her panties, easing them down her legs. Only her bra remained, and laying back down beside her, he eased the straps off her shoulders and bent to kiss her breasts again, as his fingers stroked firmly and rhythmically between her legs, and she felt herself coming.

She could feel his hardness against her, and pulled him on top of her, opening herself to him. She grabbed hold of his buttocks, pulling him into her deeply, and as she cried out his name, he exploded inside her.

"Oh my God" she whispered, breathless. "I love you so much."

He eased himself off her and his head fell back into the pillows next to hers.

"I love you too, my darling. So much. To be with you here, in the city of love, makes me complete." He looked at her intently as he stroked her hair.

"Shall I run us a bath?" he asked.

"That sounds tempting… it's a jacuzzi bath, I noticed." Rebecca smiled, stroking his face. He got up and walked to the bathroom, as she looked on at his lean, muscular physique. She heard the water running and got up from the bed, tying her hair up with a band from her cosmetic bag as she did so.

The scent of subtle bath oils wafted out of the bathroom, and she remembered the treasured Diptyque candle Shaun had bought her, which she retrieved from her bag, lit, and took into the bathroom, dimming the ceiling light as she went in.

They sat at opposite ends of the bath, legs around each other, and Shaun fiddled with the jacuzzi controls until they created a gentle whirlpool effect in the bath. The beautiful fragrance from the candle filled the room and as it flickered, shadows danced on the bathroom walls.

"So many firsts for me, Shaun. I feel like I am reborn!" She whispered, as he smiled at her, his handsome features so familiar to her, now.

"In the short time we have been together, you've given me so much joy, darling. I want every day to be perfect for you."

He reached for her hands, lifting them to his lips and kissing them. They lay in the bath for a while, and then Shaun got out and reached for the fluffy white robes, holding one out for her as she rose from the bath, her skin gleaming.

The room was pitch dark when Rebecca woke up. Looking at the clock beside the bed, she saw it was past 9am. Shaun stirred beside her.

"Good morning…" She leaned across, kissing him on his closed eyelids.

"Morning darling. How did you sleep?"

"Really well, such a comfortable bed… and you?"

"The same… do you still want to stay another night?" He said.

Rebecca nodded. "I really want to! We can spend the day exploring!" She said, enthusiastically.

While she showered and got ready, Shaun phoned the concierge and booked the room for a second night.

They went down to the restaurant for breakfast, which was a mouth-watering array of fruits, pastries, breads and hot food. Choosing a table by a large window that looked out over the river, the bright morning sun was reflected on its rippling surface; it held the promise of a beautiful day...

As they ate, Shaun a cooked breakfast of sizzling bacon, sausages and eggs, Rebecca poached eggs on sourdough toast, they planned the day ahead. First, a visit to the "Tuileries" gardens, then on to the Louvre, after which Shaun was insistent about a walk to Place Vendome.

"What's there?" Rebecca asked.

"It's a lovely square, there are some great shops. You've got to see it." He said. She feigned mock surprise, as she said, "shops? You like shopping?"

"I have to buy my fiancee a souvenir from Paris!"

After breakfast, Rebecca changed into her DKNY leatherette jeggings, a cosy grey marl sweater, and her Air Force, which she decided would be the most comfortable for walking. She tied her hair back into a low ponytail and spritzed her Byredo perfume behind her ears.

"Ready!" she called out as she came out of the bathroom.

"You look sexy, come here…" he said.

She walked over to him, and he grabbed her bottom, squeezing it with both hands. He kissed her, tasting her minty fresh breath. "Later…" he whispered in her ear… as he nibbled her earlobe. Realising she'd forgotten to put on her earrings, she pulled away gently from him and retrieved them from beside the bed. Little emerald-cut diamond studs that her parents had bought her for her twenty-first birthday, her most favourite earrings.

The walk to the "Jardins Des Tuileries" took them ten minutes, and in the bright sunshine, it felt warm. Shaun held her hand as he pointed out various landmarks that he remembered from before. As they approached the gardens, they could see the Arc de Triomphe ahead, a giant, gleaming Ferris wheel in front of it. Rebecca turned back to look at the majestic Eiffel tower behind them.

They walked through the beautiful gardens, and Shaun told Rebecca what he knew about the lavish palace that had once stood there, the residence of most French monarchs, until it burned to the ground in the 1870s. They stopped to read some historical facts displayed on placards, drawings showing what the original palace built in the 16th century would have looked like, with its different architectural styles added on over the years. Shaun explained each style to her, from Renaissance in the 17th and 18th centuries, to Baroque and then Neo-classicism in the 19th century.

"I hope I'm not boring you with my passion for buildings…" he looked at her with mock concern, one eyebrow raised.

"Not at all! It's fascinating, and your knowledge is extensive! I mean, I've heard of these periods in architecture, but I wouldn't have recognised them in buildings. Now, I think I might!" she laughed. Walking on into the gardens, they followed the "Axe historique" which the Louvre courtyard opened onto. They came to the Musee de l'Orangerie, on the Terrace de l'Orangerie where, before its entrance, Rodin's bronze sculpture, "The Kiss" rests.

"Oh my, look at this! Paola and Francesca! I've always wanted to see this! I didn't realise it was here!" Rebecca exclaimed. They stood in front of it, admiring the beauty of the bronze. "Let's have a photo of us, in front of this!" Rebecca held up her phone and captured the moment in time.

"I seem to remember reading that they were condemned to wander eternally through Hell!" Rebecca mused... "Because she fell in love with her husband's brother, and he killed them both."

"This is one of many bronzes Rodin did, of the same sculpture. The original was marble." Shaun read on the plaque. "It says Rodin's most celebrated sculpture, 'Eve' is also in these gardens."

"Over there," Rebecca pointed to a grassy area at the side of the museum.

"It represents Eve shrinking in despair, ashamed of her sin, and in anguish." Shaun reflected. Rebecca studied the bronze. "You are so knowledgeable!"

"I love art... and beauty," he said, staring at her, before pulling her into his arms and kissing her. Inside the museum, they viewed the entire series of Monet's Water Lilies.

"This place is magical." Rebecca said, almost breathless with excitement. "I've always adored these paintings... to be here, actually seeing them, is unbelievable!"

Shaun smiled. "It is amazing seeing them, especially with you! Your enthusiasm is infectious!" he said, smiling.

"Would you like to go on the Ferris wheel?" Shaun asked her.

"No, I'm not great with heights! I don't want to go up the Eiffel tower, either, I'm happy to see things from the ground. That's why I freaked out on the plane when it diverted, I've always been like it." She explained.

"That's ok, I'm not bothered about going up it, either. Probably loads of tourists, too. Shall we carry on to the Louvre?" He replied.

"Yes, we should, as it's getting late." As they walked, she realised she had not thought or talked about Nigel at all since they got to France, apart from when she had told her Mother about her sordid discovery. It was as though her old life had ceased to exist.

They headed to the Louvre, crossing the courtyard from the gardens, as the glass pyramid structure loomed before them. "This place has had so many additions, you wouldn't believe it. In the 13th and 14th centuries it was a Gothic structure, then Renaissance, finally Modernism, in the 20th century." Shaun told her. "It's so vast, we'd need a week to see it all. I think if the main painting you want to see is the 'Mona Lisa,' I checked and we should head straight to the Galerie Medici's first, then we'll find out where Venus is. I think there might be queues, though."

When they got to the Galerie Medici's, the queue wasn't too bad, probably as it was the end of the busy summer season here. They found the 'Mona Lisa' and Rebecca looked surprised when she saw how small the iconic painting was. Behind its glass casing, it wasn't easy to get too close to it, either... but it still took her breath away. She studied it as Shaun watched her reaction. It was as if there was a connection between Rebecca and it. Her eyes glistened, and Shaun took her hand. He read her a piece from the text beside the painting...

"She peacefully smiles, as the river flows on behind her. Here, the water symbolizes the 'passing of time.'"

"I'm so glad I have finally seen it." She sighed.

"The Venus de Milo is on the ground floor of the 'Sully' wing. Shall we head there now, or is there anything else you'd like to see here?" Shaun asked, after checking its location on his phone.

"Let's go straight to it, we've still so much to see after here."

They entered gallery 16 in the 'Sully' wing and there she was, upon a stand.

"Oh, how beautiful she is! And so tall, surely over six feet?"

Rebecca walked closer to the statue to read the plaque beside it.

'Venus, also believed to be Aphrodite, Goddess of Love' discovered in 1820, Melos, Greece.

Not the original marble, believed to be a Roman copy of the original Greek sculpture.'

"Oh, not the original? But anyway, this sculpture always intrigued me, especially as a child. I always wanted to know what happened to her arms!" Rebecca laughed. Shaun patted her bottom, whispering in her ear, "Your curves are a work of art."

After the Louvre, they headed out onto the "Rue de Rivoli" in search of a café for lunch. They found a traditional French place, Café Blanc, where they ordered coffee and freshly baked savoury croissants and sat at a little table outside. As Rebecca drank her coffee, she looked across at Shaun. "So, tour guide… what's next?"

"We'll walk across to Place Vendome… it's known as Paris' most beautiful neo-classical square, most famous for its "Colonne Vendome," cast from bronze from some 1200 cannons of the Austrian and Russian armies and erected by Napoleon 1, it says on Google. There are some amazing shops, too, if you wanted to look at any?"

"Normally I would jump at an offer like that, but today, it's just been so overwhelming, I want to keep everything I've seen fresh in my mind, shopping will distract me. Anyway, there's nothing I really need." Rebecca said.

"Ok, darling. There's just one place I want to take you, at 3 o'clock."

"Oh... where?"

He smiled. "Wait and see."

They walked across the street to Place Vendome, which was at the starting point of the Rue de la Paix. With its elegant buildings all the same cream-coloured stone, standing in an octagonal layout, Place Vendome was indeed lovely. The famous column stood proudly in the centre, its verdigris hue decorated in classical style with bas reliefs representing trophies, and a statue of Napoleon at the top of it.

Rebecca saw all the high-end jewellers, Boucheron, Chaumet and the new Graff flagship boutique the famous architect, Peter Marino had designed, Shaun told her.

They passed the elegant Ritz hotel, which overlooked the centre of Place Vendome, its original facade designed by the royal architect Jules Hardouin-Mansart and then updated by Charles Mewes, both of whose architecture styles Shaun had studied he told her, when he was in Paris.

"Coco Chanel lived here for over 30 years, apparently, and Elton John has a suite named after him, decorated in pink and cream… very flamboyant, I've heard. Its most lavish suites cost up to 20,000 euros a night. The Imperial suite was where Princess Diana had her last meal, with Dodi Fayed. It's as a National Monument of France, now." Shaun told her.

"Al Fayed still owns it, doesn't he?" Rebecca asked.

"Yes, he bought it in '79 in a state of serious decline, for some $20 million. It took 10 years of renovation, headed by an architect called Bernard Gaucherel, who I was fortunate enough to have worked alongside once, on another massive hotel project. Anyway, it ended up costing $250 million! Then in 2016 it had a major fire. You might remember? "

"I do! It was just due to reopen after all the years of renovation, wasn't it?"

"It was a major setback, but at least the building was unoccupied, so it injured no one." Shaun replied.

"We could have a drink there later, if you'd like? They say the Ritz bar could have been the world's first ever cocktail bar… and there's Bar Hemingway, named after the author himself when he claimed it was his favourite bar, so the story goes."

"Oh yes, I'd love to see inside, let's do that!" Rebecca said excitedly. The Ritz… who'd have thought? She wondered what Lucy and Mia would say. Shaun checked the time on his beloved vintage Piaget watch, and, seeing it was nearly 3pm, grabbed Rebecca's hand.

"Come, we've got an appointment!" He said, grabbing her hand.

"Where?" she asked.

"Tiffany's!"

She looked at him, shocked, as she followed him onto Rue de la Paix. The art déco style store, with its stone facade and "Tiffany & Co" signage in silver, was across the square in front of them. A liveried doorman at the entrance held open the door for them, ushering them into a foyer with marble flooring and elegant pillars on either side. An attractive woman appeared, in a smart navy suit and high-heeled court shoes.

"May I help, Madame, Monsieur?" she said, in excellent English.

"We have an appointment at 3pm." Said Shaun, impatiently.

'Ah, you must be Mr. Forsythe, non?"

"Yes, and Ms. Rodgers."

"Please, follow me." She turned and walked into an enormous room, her heels clicking on the marble floor.

This, the main jewellery hall, had huge glass cabinets displaying dazzling gems, the chandeliers hanging from the high, ornate ceiling sparkled brightly above them.

"I am Monique. I shall assist you today. Please, we shall go into this room."

She opened a heavy-looking oak panelled door at the rear of the main hall which led into a smaller, panelled room. An ornate, carved desk with two wing-backed chairs upholstered in turquoise velvet were in front of it, which she motioned to, as she pulled out one for herself from behind the desk.

Shaun and Rebecca sat down and Monique offered them tea, coffee or champagne.

"Champagne, darling?"

Rebecca nodded, feeling overwhelmed at the ostentation surrounding her. Monique left the room, and Shaun leaned across to her.

"Are you ok?" he asked, concerned.

"Are we here for what I think we are?" She asked him quietly.

"To get your engagement ring, yes. Tiffany rings are modern and sexy, like you, but timeless too. I thought it would be a lovely surprise for you? There are plenty of other jewellery places in Place Vendome, you saw that, but I think you'll find something you love, here? If you don't, we can always leave?" He looked worried now, his usual self- assuredness not as apparent.

Rebecca took his hand. "I'm not being ungrateful, I'm just worried about the cost of everything! You haven't let me contribute for anything, since we met! You mustn't think I'm a... a woman who just lets the man pay for everything! I have money, and I can support myself, or at least pay my way! I just want you to know that."

"Darling, we're getting married! I want to support you, give you everything you need and more! And I want you to have a ring that means the world to you, that you can't stop looking at, that reflects your beauty inside and out! That's why I chose this place, but if you aren't sure, we'll go, find somewhere else? It's totally your choice." He looked at her earnestly. She shook her head. "No, it's ok. You've gone to the trouble to arrange it. I will have a look, but I don't need anything ridiculously expensive." She replied, as she took his hand in hers. Monique returned with two glasses of champagne for them. Rebecca took one from the tray, took a sip, and tried to relax.

"Shall we begin?" Monique asked.

Rebecca nodded. "We'd like to see your engagement rings." Shaun said.

"Of course. Now, we have to decide the shape you like first?" Monique asked.

Rebecca looked at her hands… she hadn't a clue. "Could you show me a selection, please?" she asked.

"Of course, Madame." Monique picked up the phone on the desk and spoke to someone in rapid French.

A few moments later, a young sales associate appeared, with white-gloved hands, holding a black velvet board with a small selection of rings on it.

"These are our most classic, yet modern designs, Madame."

As she looked at them, a simple, yet brilliant, square diamond on a silver band caught her eye.

"I like this one." She pointed at the one she'd chosen.

"Ah, yes, Madame. May I measure your ring finger, so you can try it in your size, if we 'ave it?"

Rebecca held out her left hand, which had been bare of her wedding ring since she first met Shaun. Monique produced a set of ring sizers and immediately found the right size for Rebecca. Picking up the phone and speaking quickly again, she smiled across at Rebecca. "We do 'ave this one in your size, in stock! This is quite unusual Madame, normally we 'ave to order them." The same young man appeared, this time with the chosen ring in its turquoise box, on the board of black velvet. Shaun picked up the box, and, taking the ring out, turned to Rebecca.

"May I?" he asked.

Giggling nervously, she held out her hand and Shaun slid the ring onto her finger. Rebecca looked at it and took a sharp intake of breath as he watched her reaction, and Monique smiled knowingly.

The diamond sparkled under the chandelier above them, its design exactly as Shaun had described, modern and sexy, and very Rebecca.

"So, this is our .25 carat Emerald-cut engagement ring, in platinum, which is equal to 0.47 of a carat. VS1 in its clarity, H in its colour, and the cut is excellent. A wonderful choice, and it looks lovely on your hand, Madame. All of our diamonds are sourced responsibly from mines in Botswana, Namibia and South Africa. We as a company 'ave a zero-tolerance policy towards conflict diamonds." Monique told them, as she stood and said, "I shall leave you alone for a little while."

"What do you think, darling?" Shaun asked, taking her hand and admiring the ring.

"I've never seen anything as beautiful in my life." Rebecca replied, tears in her eyes. She looked at him, smiling through her tears.

"It fits with your beauty, my love. If you are happy with it, I would like you to have it… unless you want to keep looking, just in case?"

"No, this is the one. And look, it complements my earrings!" She held her left hand up to her ear, to show him.

"It does, indeed." He leant in towards her and kissed her gently, rubbing the ring on her hand.

They left Tiffany's, Rebecca wearing the ring. Squinting as they walked out into bright sunshine, it sparkled as she held out her hand to look at it.

"Let's get a photo, for Mum and Dad?" Rebecca said. Shaun got his phone out, and she held her hand up to her face, the ring glittering as he took the picture. She looked at it after he'd taken it, and she didn't recognise herself. Who was this carefree young… yes, young woman in the picture? Her honey blonde hair framed her face flatteringly, her eyes looked bright, her lips full and rosy, and her skin a golden brown from the few days in the sun. In the picture, Shaun was looking at her, smiling down at her. It was a lovely photo. She sent it to her parents, now installed in Shaun's contacts, and wrote:

"Notice anything? Love R xx "

It was 5.30pm, a reasonable time to head to the Ritz for a celebratory drink at Hemingway's Bar, they decided. As they approached the hotel, the liveried doorman held open the glass door of one of the four entrances, and they walked in. The lobby had a plush red carpet laid on shiny cream marble tiled floors, a high ornate ceiling with elaborate cornices, and a sweeping staircase with beautiful wrought iron balustrades leading up to the floors above. It was a traditional interior, but with a modern twist. A concierge directed them to the bar, just beyond the shopping gallery. It wasn't open until 6pm, but the barman welcomed them in and showed them to a cosy, intimate table in an alcove.

The bar was much smaller than Rebecca had expected, with Hemingway memorabilia lining the wood-panelled walls. There were photos, handwritten letters from

Hemingway to his wife on Ritz letter headed paper, documents, book-covers. There was not an inch of wood panelling left without something to do with Hemingway on it, it was a fantastic homage to the great man himself.

The long serving head-barman, who introduced himself as Colin Field, asked them whether it was a special occasion. Rebecca felt herself blush, as she said, "We just got engaged..." Colin, in his white dinner jacket, his name embroidered on its pocket, regarded Rebecca thoughtfully.

"Congratulations to you both! I have the perfect drink for you, Madame. And Sir, will you let me make the same for you?" He enquired.

"Why not?" Shaun seemed happy to let Colin make a fuss of Rebecca.

Colin reappeared with two interesting looking cocktails, which he placed down on the table for them. He lay a pale pink rose next to Rebecca's drink. Shaun held his glass to Rebecca's, and they sipped the cocktails, as he waited, expectantly.

"Delicious, what is in it?" asked Rebecca.

"This is our Ritz Pimms. It has many secret ingredients, including the obvious ones: champagne, of course, and ginger ale." He said, leaving them with a wink and a smile, as the bar became busier with new customers. The cocktails looked as lovely as they tasted, with their garnishes of cucumber, mint and griottine cherries.

Rebecca held her coupe glass up to Shaun's. "Thank you for a wonderful day, and for my beautiful ring." she said, smiling, as she admired it on her hand.

"Thank you... for spending it with me, and for becoming my fiancée...

officially!" he leaned towards her, kissing her slowly and deeply. She tasted the cocktail on his lips as she responded, her tongue sensuously licking the sweetness off them. Shaun's phone buzzed, and a message from her parents popped up on the screen.

"Good timing… I won't be able to stand up in a minute!" He groaned, softly. She laughed, her hand sliding under the table as she felt for him. He read the text;

"Looks like you've been shopping? Beautiful ring, congratulations! Hope you're having a wonderful time, we really miss you being here! Xx"

Colin came over to check on them, and they ordered two more of the same cocktails. He returned with olives, warm almonds and perfectly cut crisps to accompany the drinks. Rebecca felt lightheaded and leant against Shaun as he bent and kissed her head.

"We'd better get some dinner soon?" he suggested. "Yes, we had! Or I shall be completely drunk!" Rebecca giggled. They finished their drinks, and as much as Colin tried to encourage them to stay for his special "Dirty Martini" cocktails, they said their goodbyes and strolled back to their hotel. Darkness had fallen, but the bright city lights twinkled, lighting up the sky with a golden haze...

When they got back to their room, Rebecca kicked her trainers off and flopped on to the bed, as she sighed. "What a fabulous day! I am exhausted! Are you?" she lifted herself onto one elbow, looking across the room as Shaun took his boots off. Rebecca lay back into the soft pillows and closed her eyes as Shaun dimmed the lights. Hearing the bath running and smelling delicious bath oils wafting into the room, she felt as though she was floating outside her body. Then she could hear Shaun on the phone, but she couldn't make out his words.

"Darling?" Shaun whispered, and she jumped. "Oh, I must have drifted off! That was the most delightful feeling!" She said sleepily. "I've run us a bath, and then I've booked a table for dinner, somewhere really nice." He said, stroking her cheek gently. "Where?" She asked, as she stretched her arms above her head, sighing.

"Le Relais Plaza, in the hotel Plaza d'Athenee. It's a must see here, as famous for the art deco interior as its food: if you're not too tired? It's our last night here, I want it to be really special." He said, as he gently undressed her. "No, I'm not too tired, but what shall I wear? Is it really posh?" She asked, worried as she was running out of clean clothes. "You could wear the black dress? I love that on you." He said as she walked to the bathroom, and slipped into the luxurious, foaming bath. As she rested her head back, she called out to him.

"Are you going to join me?"

He stood in the doorway and smiling at her sexily, he slipped his jeans off, then his shorts. He climbed into the bath and sat opposite her, his legs around her. She lifted herself up onto her knees and leaned over him, placing her hands underneath his buttocks and lifting him into her mouth as he laid his head back on the rim of the bath. He groaned with pleasure as she sucked and licked him, loving the way he grew harder as she did so. He shuddered, coming forcefully as he cried out her name.

"Christ, Rebecca. You are a sexy woman. Jesus!" He said, as he looked at her. She smiled, "That was to say thank you for my ring!"

The taxi swerved in and out of the busy evening traffic, taking them to the

Montaigne address. Shaun told her how the design of the restaurant was modelled on the SS Normandie, otherwise known as 'the ship of light.'

Her lavish Art deco style on board had given her the title of the greatest ocean liner, and they had recreated that style in the restaurant. As they walked in, Rebecca gasped at the sheer beauty of it. It almost had an old theatrical feel to it, with its golden charm and deco chandeliers. Shown to an elegantly dressed table, Shaun ordered a bottle of Cristal champagne for them, and gazed at Rebecca.

"How beautiful you look tonight, my love." He said quietly, reaching for her hand.

"Thank you. This *is* a perfect end to our trip, you were right." She smiled, sipping her champagne.

They both ordered the beef tartare, head chef Alain Ducasse's signature dish, which arrived served with grilled artichokes and fries. After the meal, they wandered back out onto the now quiet Paris streets. "Do you want to walk for a bit?" Shaun asked.

"Yes, let us. It's not so far back, is it?" Rebecca asked, as he slipped his arm around her waist.

"No, probably fifteen minutes' walk?"

They slowly walked back towards the hotel, as they talked about leaving the next day.

"So, tomorrow, there's a Eurostar leaving at 3.15pm, shall we get that… gets us into London by 6pm?"

"Yes, that sounds ok, at least we can have a leisurely morning that way." Rebecca replied.

"What's the plan when we get back?" she asked, feeling sudden doubts creeping in. She didn't want to go back to London, didn't want this precious time to end. He noticed the look on her face change to one of worry.

"Don't you be worrying, now. It's all going to work out fine. We'll have a few days in London, clear the flat completely, tie up some loose ends, then we'll head to Dublin. I had arranged to stay with an old friend, just outside the city. How would you feel about that? His name is Declan… his wife died a couple of years ago, and I've not seen him since then. When he found out I was moving back, he made me promise to stop and see him on my way. Of course, that was before I met you. So, if you don't mind, I'll tell him about you, and that you will be with me. Is that ok?"

"That sounds fine, if you think *he* won't mind? I've not seen much of Dublin, I always wanted to stop there, but we never did. My Dad was always in such a rush to get on the road to Aunt Norah's." Rebecca smiled, remembering her Dad's terrible driving, and how she and Andrea had always felt carsick!

Chapter 12.

London.

The Eurostar nosed its way out of 'Gare du Nord' station slowly, leaving behind a grey, drizzly Paris. Rebecca looked out of the window, sad that their precious time there had ended, but filled with anticipation for the next chapter of their new life together. She knew there would be some awkward phone calls in the next few days, to the solicitor and Nigel. Shaun squeezed her hand, gently. "Penny for them?" he whispered.

"Oh, just sad to be leaving! I've had such a wonderful time here, with you. And I'm not looking forward to the calls I have to make, tomorrow."

"I know. But once they're out of the way, we can get on with things, move forward."

It was raining in London too, the daylight fading into a damp, chilly evening. Shaun put his arm around Rebecca as they left St. Pancras station and waited for a black cab to take them to Islington. Once there, Shaun opened the door to his flat, a cleverly converted dwelling in a Victorian terraced house, and they went in.

Rebecca had not seen inside it when they left her suitcases here, on their way to France. It was more or less empty now, just a couple of cases belonging to Shaun, and her forlorn looking ones, holding just a few remnants of her old life.

Shaun picked up the mail that lay on the doormat, checked around quickly, and put their cases into the waiting cab. He locked up the flat for the last time, posting the key back through the letterbox. They climbed into the cab, and the driver took them across town to the Hilton London Angel, which Shaun had pre-booked that morning.

The hotel was contemporary, and right in the heart of the lively shopping and entertainment hub that was the Angel. Pleased with their room, which was spacious, clean and had a view of the London Eye and the Tower of London, Rebecca said, "This is great, Shaun! A really excellent location..." She was feeling more positive than she had been earlier.

"It's a great area, lots of good restaurants and bars, and Sadler's Wells is right here too... we could see what's on maybe?" he replied.

"You would see a ballet?" she asked, realising there was so much about him she didn't know yet.

"Like I told you, I love beauty... and art... and you." He swept her up into his arms and carried her to the king-size bed. "And you've driven me crazy with longing, all day!" he groaned, as he lowered her onto the bed, and then himself on top of her.

He nuzzled her neck, and she couldn't help but giggle as his soft stubble tickled her cheek. He slowly undressed her, kissing her all over. She reached for the buckle on his jeans, undid it and deftly unbuttoned his fly, pushing them down over his hips as she guided him into her.

"Let's find somewhere nice for dinner?" he said, as he stroked her naked shoulder and kissed her. "I've worked up an appetite!"

"Mmm, me too. I fancy spicy? Maybe a curry or something?" Rebecca replied, stretching out against his lean nakedness.

"There's an Indian near here, Memsaab, I've not tried it, but I've heard the food is superb."

As Rebecca showered, Shaun booked a table for them at the Indian, and then checked the Sadler's website. Amazingly, the English National Ballet were performing "Giselle" the following evening. He called out to Rebecca, asking if he should book it, as there were only limited seats available now.

"Fabulous! Yes, please do!" She answered back.

She came out of the bathroom, as Shaun was making the booking, and wondered what to wear for dinner.

"All done, good seats, too!" He smiled across at her.

"I'm running out of clean clothes... we must use the hotel laundry while we're here? I don't know what to wear tonight... or tomorrow, to the ballet?" she said.

"Yes, I need some clean stuff too. Let's send it off tomorrow morning. Why not wear your grey cashmere sweater tonight... and those sexy leggings? I love you in that." He said, looking over at her.

She unpacked her case, finding the clothes he'd suggested. As he showered, she got ready, applying her makeup carefully and blow drying her hair. Perhaps she should go shopping tomorrow, get a few more clothes before they left for Ireland. Looking at herself in the mirror, she was pleased with her reflection. He made her feel beautiful, just by the way he looked at her. Holding her hand up to admire her ring, it sparkled back at her and she felt a sudden sob rising in her throat. This all seemed like a dream, a wonderful dream that she didn't want to wake up from.

They walked to the restaurant, as the streets were filling with evening revellers. The atmosphere was lively, the London sky brightly lit, casting a glow over the city. The servers welcomed them as they walked into

'Memsaab' and showed them to a table by the window, looking out on to the hustle and bustle of the Angel. Shaun ordered wine for them, and they looked at the menus. "I'm going for hot... king prawn jalfrezi, I think." Rebecca said. Shaun chose a lamb madras, as they shared the poppadums and pickles the waiter had brought with their wine.

"This might be your last curry for a while... no Indian takeaways near Lough Rosslaire!" Shaun commented, a wry smile on his handsome face.

"I make quite a mean curry... if I can get all the ingredients there?" she said, curiously.

"Perhaps we should get them in Dublin. There are a few Asian cash & carry stores in the city... they just haven't spread out to the counties, yet! But I shall look forward to your cooking, no doubt another hidden talent of yours?" he smiled, taking her hand and stroking her long fingers. "How are you liking your ring?" he asked.

"I adore my ring. I've never owned anything so gorgeous."

The waiter arrived with their food, and the delightful aromas filled the air.

As they ate, Shaun talked about his time living in Islington, although he didn't mention Renee.

Rebecca was glad, she didn't want to imagine Shaun with anyone else, now. He asked her if she was looking forward to seeing 'Giselle.'

"It's such a sad story! I'll probably cry... but yes, I'm really looking forward to it, especially as the English National are performing it."

"Tell me the story?" he asked.

"Well, it's a love story. Giselle is a peasant girl who loves to dance, but she has a weak heart. In a nutshell, she falls in love with a philandering Count, Albrecht, who pretends to be a local villager to win her love. When he betrays her with another, she has a fit of madness and dances herself to death. But then, her ghost forgives him, and protects him from evil spirits called the 'Wilis,' supernatural women who died before their own wedding day, and dance men to their death as a form of spiritual justice. She disappears into the forest, he pursues her, and the 'Wilis' surround him and sentence him to death, but she saves him."

"Beautifully told, darling! How do you know it so well?"

"I had to study it, for my ballet theory exam at school. It will make me sad, but only temporarily! I'm sure you will cheer me up, afterwards..." she looked at him suggestively, a pinkish blush staining her cheeks.

After dinner, they wandered alongside the river. The evening was cool and fresh with a hint of autumn in the air. The Thames was busy, boats sailing by in both directions, their lights twinkling and the gentle hum of their motors just audible above the traffic noise.

"So, tomorrow… I have a few calls to make, possibly a meeting: I can do that after breakfast. What do you need to do, darling?" Shaun asked her, as they walked, hand in hand.

"I need to talk to the solicitor, and then I'll send Nigel an email, just to make sure they've updated him… I don't want to call him. I must also get in touch with my sister. And I need to do a bit of shopping… is it any good, round here?"

"Yes, the shops are alright. The ballet is at 7.30pm, so shall we have dinner after?" he said. They strolled back to the hotel leisurely, as Rebecca made a mental list of things she needed to buy.

In the middle of the night, she was woken with a start, her phone buzzing beside the bed. She looked at the time... 1.45 am! Picking up her phone; she saw the text. It was from Nigel:

"Where are you, Rebecca? I miss you. I'm sorry for everything. So sorry, X"

Placing the phone back down on the bedside table, she thought what now? He had left her alone the last few weeks. Why was he bothering her at this time in the morning? He must be drunk, she thought. Shaun stirred next to her, reaching out for her. She pressed herself back into him as she tried to go back to sleep. An unbearable sadness crept over her, and she tossed and turned most of the night, disturbed by the message.

While Shaun made her tea in the morning, she told him about the text.

"I just don't know why he's contacting me now, it has been weeks!" she said anxiously.

"Try not to read too much into it, darling. Find out the status quo from your solicitor, take it from there. I'm here, if you need me." Shaun reassured her, as he always did. He brought her tea to her and sat down on the bed next to her. She sipped it, feeling calmer.

"Shall we go for breakfast? That will make you feel better!" He smiled, stroking her shoulder.

After they had eaten, Shaun got on with making his calls. Rebecca brushed her teeth and got on with what she needed to do before she went out shopping. Shaun was busy on his laptop, so she sat by the window and dialled the solicitor first.

"Susan Clark, please." She said, as the Down & Co receptionist answered.

"Just putting you through, one moment. May I ask who's calling?"

"Mrs… Rebecca Rodgers."

"Good morning, Susan Clark. How may I help?"

"Good morning, it's Mrs..er, Rebecca Rodgers. I just wanted to know how things are progressing, as I haven't heard from you?"

"We served papers 2 weeks ago, and I believe we received them, signed by the respondent, yesterday. Therefore, the Decree Nisi should happen fairly quickly now, Mrs. Rodgers."

"So how long will it be for the entire process to be completed?"

"It usually takes six weeks after acknowledgement of the Decree Nisi for the issue of the Decree Absolute."

"Oh, ok. Is Mr. Rodgers being kept up to date with the proceedings?"

"Yes, the respondent has been receiving all the necessary documentation and is compliant. Is there anything else I can help you with?"

"I'm leaving the country, so could you please ensure I receive regular emails regarding any updates I need to know about?"

"Yes, of course, I will make a note of that on your file. Do you have a forwarding address?"

"No, not yet. I will only be contactable by email."

"Ah, that's fine. Goodbye, Mrs. Rodgers."

"Thank you, goodbye." She ended the call and sighed heavily.

Shaun looked across the room, an eyebrow raised. She shook her hand and mouthed "okay" to him.

Next, she sent Nigel an email.

Hi Nigel.

I hope you are well. It surprised me to see a text from you last night, especially at such a late hour. Please refrain from contacting me in this way.

I have spoken to the solicitor and everything is proceeding smoothly, so thank you for completing the paperwork. They have said they should complete the Decree Absolute in six weeks.

I am leaving England the day after tomorrow, for Ireland. I shall let the boys know my new address. I have everything I want from the house. Please let me know by email when you have decided what to do about the house.

Look after yourself,

Rebecca.

As she reread it to herself, she thought it sounded ok, not too harsh. Pretty final... but that's what she wanted. An end to it. Shaun brought her over a coffee.

"Are you ok, darling?" he asked.

"Yes, I am. We're looking at another six weeks, before it's all finalised. I just emailed Nigel, asked him not to text me again." she replied. Shaun bent and kissed her head. "What time do you want to hit the shops? I have to meet my old boss as he wants to talk to me about freelance work." he said.

"I'm just going to call Andrea, see when they are free to meet up, then I'll be ready."

Andrea answered after a couple of rings, sounding harassed. "Hello?"

"It's Rebecca!" she said, surprised that her number obviously hadn't come up on Andrea's phone. "Are you ok?"

"Hi Becs. I'm just knackered, you know, work… kids… Anyway, it's been a while since we've spoken! How are you?"

Rebecca felt a sudden rush of guilt. She hadn't really kept Andrea in the loop at all, and now she was about to drop a bombshell on her big sister. She'd better play it all down a bit, she decided.

She told her about leaving Nigel, and Dark Rain, and moving to Ireland with Shaun. She mentioned they'd visited their parents in France, leaving out the Paris adventure.

"Oh my God! Are you sure about him? How long have you known each other? What did Mum and Dad say? What about the boys?" Andrea's words came tumbling out in a breathless bombardment.

"I thought we could meet… tomorrow, if that suits you? I can fill you in then… and you can meet Shaun?"

"Tomorrow... I don't know. I'll talk to Harry, call you back."

"Ok, talk to you later, then." Rebecca felt hurt as she ended the call, but she guessed Andrea was just being over-protective.

As she wandered round the local shops, she realised it was the first time she'd been on her own for weeks. It felt strange, slightly unnerving. Shaun had taken a tube to Victoria to meet his old boss, and she didn't like him not being with her.

Finding a Zara store, she bought a few basics; sweatshirts and t-shirts, jeans and jumpers. There was a Cotswold Co. shop, where she found a practical waterproof Barbour wax jacket, and black short wellies. In Reiss, she bought a gorgeous black velvet tux, and a cream silk tie neck blouse, perfect for the ballet tonight, she thought. Then she stocked up on underwear from Intimissimi, and a couple of pairs of their thermal leatherette leggings, and some gorgeous silk pyjamas. There was a Dune store, and she thought she'd buy some high heels, not that she'd probably need them much in Ireland. Still, a pair for dressing up in tonight would be good. Finding court shoes in calf skin leopard print, and a little matching cross body bag, she couldn't resist purchasing them. Toiletries from Boots, including a deep red lipstick, bought on a whim, and she'd finished.

Making her way back to the hotel, she stopped at a hair salon and made an appointment for highlights for the following morning, realising it had been weeks since she had last had her hair done. Pleased with all she'd accomplished, even choosing two cable knit sweaters in Superdry that were perfect for Shaun, she arrived back at the hotel. He was just walking up the street as she got there, and she smiled. "I've missed you," she said, as she kissed him.

"And you, darling. You look like you've had a successful trip! Let me take those for you." He took the bags off her, and they went up to their room. Shaun made her tea while she showed him what she'd bought.

"I shall look forward to seeing you in these," he said, picking up the pretty lingerie she'd laid out on the bed.

"Oh, and I bought these for you…" she handed him the Superdry bag. "For me? You didn't have to do that!" Shaun opened the bag and pulled out the jumpers. "These are nice, just what I'd have chosen. Thank you, darling!" he said, trying the navy one first, then the camel. Both suited his dark complexion. He kissed her and asked her if she'd like a bath run.

"I guess I'd better get ready, I didn't realise the time!" she said, as she laid out her clothes for the evening. When the bath was ready, she lay back in the foamy water, whilst he told her about his meeting.

"I've a lot of freelance work lined up, so it was worth the meeting. I'll arrange delivery of all my work stuff, my desk and equipment and everything, just before we move into the house. It's in storage in Dublin at the moment." He seemed excited.

"Where will you put your workstation?" she asked, thinking about the layout of the house. "At the front window, looking out to sea, initially. Then once we're in, I'll decide where I want my permanent office to be." He replied.

"Oh yes, best to live there for a bit, then decide... see where the light is best, I guess?" she closed her eyes, thinking about the monumental move she was making.

"Said like a true architect!" Shaun laughed as he kissed her.

He let out a low whistle when he saw her outfit.

"You look stunning." he said.

Rebecca blushed. "Thank you." The cream silk blouse, slashed suggestively at the front, became demure by its elegantly tied scarf at the neck. The black velvet tux, one satin button fastened at the middle, complemented it beautifully. She wore her new leather leggings, and the leopard print heels. She'd put her hair up into a French twist, and applied the red lipstick, keeping the rest of her makeup natural. Silver hoop earrings with pearl droplets finished the look.

Shaun had put on a floral navy Ted Baker shirt, his dark jeans and her favourite tweed jacket. They headed down to the hotel bar for a drink before the ballet and then walked the short distance from the hotel to the Sadler's Wells theatre.

Shaun had secretly booked a private box, with a perfect view of the stage. Thrilled, Rebecca took her seat next to him and the ballet began.

The lights dimmed, and 'Giselle' danced onto the stage, alone, for Act 1, with its historical detail and rustic colour, and the famous 'mad scene,' in which she dies. Rebecca's eyes filled with tears as the beautiful Giselle danced herself to her death and Act 1 ended.

During the interval, they went to the bar for a drink. Shaun ordered wine for them, and they stood looking out onto the busy streets below them.

"Are you enjoying it?" she asked him.

"I'm enjoying watching you. It transfixes you."

"It's so beautiful. It... expresses the most important thing in life!" she whispered.

"Love." He replied, as he stroked her face.

"Yes, love."

Act II was dramatically different. The stage had become a moonlit, ethereal forest, where the 'Wilis' dancers, one of which Giselle had now become, haunted their prey. Rebecca leant forward, mesmerised by the mystical, otherworldly dancing.

The ten dancers on stage were all in white, with white veils covering their faces. As the lead male dancer, Albrecht, danced into the 'Wilis' trap, Giselle saved him from them, and in doing so, released her soul from their power.

The ballet ended, and Rebecca dabbed her eyes and looked across at Shaun. He smiled, squeezing her hand. They left the theatre and headed out on to the still crowded streets. Rebecca, taller now in her heels, huddled into Shaun.

"Thank you so much for arranging that. I absolutely adored it." she said.

"I could see that, and I did, too. For an absolute ballet heathen, I've surprised myself! Now, I booked Ottolenghi's for dinner, is that ok?"

"Wow, yes! I've always wanted to try his food... and I'm starving!"

"Me too, come on, it's just up the street."

Chapter 13.

London.

The next morning, Rebecca had a text from her sister, inviting them for dinner that evening at their house in Teddington. As they ate breakfast, she told Shaun about the invitation.

"Of course, I don't mind! She's bound to want to know everything, I guess?" he said.

"Oh, she will alright, especially if she has spoken to Mum, in the meantime!" Rebecca replied. She felt slightly awkward about going, but knew she had to.

Shaun walked her to the hairdressers, arranging to meet for lunch after her appointment. Having the time whilst her hair was being done to just sit and think about everything, Rebecca felt slightly sad at the thought of leaving England, and all that was familiar. But then she reminded herself how her life here had more or less ground to a halt, and that change had needed to happen. She certainly didn't feel she was acting impulsively, but no doubt Andrea would make her feel that way.

Shaun was outside the salon when she came out. He took her in his arms, saying, "Wow, your hair looks lovely, darling," as he did so. The hairdresser had done a good job, giving Rebecca caramel and honey face framing highlights that complemented her olive complexion. She'd also cut some swishy layers in, which fell flatteringly to Rebecca's shoulders.

"Shall we just go back to the hotel?" Shaun asked, a twinkle in his eye. Rebecca felt her cheeks burn as she said, "You are insatiable… and I'm hungry... but maybe after?" She replied, laughing.

Shaun suggested the "Narrowboat" pub, which was the only Islington pub right on the Regent's canal, close to Angel station. The sun had come out, and, for October, it was pleasantly warm. They sat outside, overlooking the canal, and the waitress brought their drinks over. They both ordered the fresh fish catch of the day, and, as they waited for the food to come, they sat enjoying the sun shining on their faces, and contemplated the afternoon ahead...

Back at the hotel after lunch, Shaun drew the curtains as Rebecca undressed and climbed into bed. He undressed, and, kneeling before her, kissed and teased her most intimate place as she squirmed beneath his tongue, softly moaning. As she came close to climax, he took hold of her hips, pulling her onto him as she threw her head back, arching her back. He thrust into her forcefully until they shuddered into each other, falling back into the pillows. They lay, breathing heavily into each other, as he said, "I love you so much, I just want you more every day." She ran her fingers through his thick, black hair, pulling him closer as she whispered, "I love you too…"

They arrived at Andrea's at 7.30. The train had taken half an hour, with a short walk from the station to the street she and Harry lived in. Andrea opened the door, excitement had replaced the harassed tone she'd greeted Rebecca with, the day before.

"Oh, my God! So good to see you! You look so well!" She exclaimed, hugging her sister. "And you must be Shaun?" as she held out her hand to greet him. Harry hovered behind her as Andrea ushered them in.

"Pleased to meet you, Shaun." he said as he shook Shaun's hand vigorously. They walked through to the large open-plan kitchen, and Andrea asked what they'd like to drink.

"We've brought Prosecco, and a few beers." Shaun said, handing a bag to Harry.

"Oh, lovely, and they're cold!" Harry said, as he took the bag from Shaun.

"The kids will down in a bit, so tell us all about how you met before they arrive, or we'll never get a word in!"

Rebecca noticed Andrea checking Shaun out, as she gestured to the bar stools at the kitchen island. Rebecca recounted the story of their meeting, as Andrea's eyes widened.

"And you're engaged?" she said, as she glanced at Rebecca's hand, taking in the beautiful ring.

"Oh my, that's impressive!" she said, as she took Rebecca's hand in hers, to look more closely at the ring.

"And you're leaving? When?" she asked.

"Well, actually, tomorrow." Rebecca said, reaching for Shaun's hand.

Andrea and Harry's teenagers, Molly and Jack, joined them for supper. They all sat at the long table in the kitchen, and Andrea served up the huge lasagne she'd made. Shaun told them a bit about the house in Ireland, inviting them to visit when they could. Molly asked Rebecca pointedly how her cousins were, looking at Shaun suspiciously. Harry said little at all, and as Rebecca helped clear the plates after dinner, she asked Andrea if everything was ok between them.

"Well, to be honest, we haven't been getting along that well for some time now. Harry has a lot of pressure at work and brings it home with him, and money is tight. I'm not sure where it's heading, really." Andrea sighed. "So good luck to you, Becs, I mean that. I know you've had a hard time with Nigel, but you're lucky you've found a way out of it... Shaun seems really lovely. As long as you aren't jumping out of the frying pan into the fire!" she said, anxiously.

"No, I'm not, Andi." Rebecca replied. "I've never been more certain about what I'm doing in my life."

Chapter 14.

Dublin.

The plane taxied along the runway towards its stand, Dublin greeting them with a foggy grey drizzle. While they waited in the baggage hall for their cases Shaun sent Declan a text, letting him know they had landed. Hailing a taxi outside the airport, Shaun told the driver the Malahide address.

"It is about 9 miles, now. Should take a half hour, maybe." The driver said, in a thick Dublin accent, as he looked at Shaun through narrowed eyes. As he weaved his way out of the heavy airport traffic, and headed towards the M50, Rebecca noticed him glancing in the rear-view mirror, frequently. Shaun held Rebecca's hand, squeezing it lightly.

"You'll like Declan, he's very easy-going, entertaining, too. It was tragic when he lost his wife, she was only 52." He told her. Rebecca asked how they'd met, and Shaun told her how they had worked on plans for Battersea Power Station together, for McAlpine. Then McAlpine had lost the contract to convert the old power station, and they never used all the plans Declan and Shaun worked so hard on, but a powerful bond forged between them, and they'd kept in regular contact over the years.

"That was a few years ago, now. I've visited him here, before. It's a beautiful house, and it's close to Malahide Castle, which is a lovely 12th-century castle, well worth seeing." Shaun said, as the taxi pulled into the long, sweeping driveway that led to Declan's house. He paid the taxi driver with a generous tip, thanking him for carrying their cases, and Rebecca noticed him looking at Shaun curiously again, as if he recognised him.

Declan's house was indeed beautiful. A New England colonial style place, with white cladding and cedar roof tiles. Wide steps led up to the large, sage green front door, with its pewter knocker. Shaun knocked, and a maid opened the door in a black uniform and white apron. Surprised, Rebecca hesitated; she had never met anyone who employed a maid before.

"Hello, Mr. Forsythe? I am Kitty. Mr. O'Donnell is in the library. Please come in, I'll fetch your cases to your room."

"Thank you, Kitty. Nice to see you again. This is Rebecca, and please, call me Shaun."

She looked slightly embarrassed and nodded. "I will, sir."

Kitty led them down a wide hallway to the library and showed them in. Declan stood up from behind a large walnut desk, coming round to greet them.

"Shaun, my old fellow. Good to see you again! And this must be the lovely lady you were telling me about. Rebecca, is it not?"

They shook hands energetically, and then Declan extended a hand to Rebecca, and, as she took it, he lifted her hand to his mouth and kissed it. She felt her cheeks glowing, and she smiled.

"Lovely to meet you, Declan." she said, as she took in the impressionable man before her. She thought he must be about sixty-eight, his salt and pepper hair and moustache placing him around that age. His eyes were the brightest cobalt blue she'd ever seen, and she could tell he would have been a particularly handsome young man. Framed photographs were everywhere around the library, on side-tables, windowsills and on the walls. Most were of a beautiful woman with jet black hair, many featuring Declan and the woman in various exotic looking locations.

"They are all of Christobel, my darling wife." He said, noticing Rebecca looking around at them. "We loved to travel."

Declan motioned to a huge leather Chesterfield sofa in front of the fireplace for them to sit on, ringing a little bell on his desk as they did so. Asleep on the hearth were two of the most enormous dogs Rebecca had ever seen. "Oh, my goodness! Who are these two?" she exclaimed, as Shaun laughed. "Duke and Duchess, my beloved wolfhounds." Declan replied, smiling.

"Now, what can I offer you? Coffee? Brandy? Wine?" he asked, as Kitty re-entered the room in response to the bell. "Oh, I'd love some tea, please." Rebecca said. Shaun said he would have the same, and Declan asked Kitty to prepare some. They sat in the library, chatting, until the old Grandfather clock in the corner chimed 6 times.

"I'll get Kitty to show you your room, you must want a wee rest before dinner? It's normally served at 7pm, if that suits you?" Declan asked.

"That's grand, thank you." Shaun stood, and Rebecca followed. Kitty silently appeared at the door and led them up a wide oak staircase to a huge landing, doors either side all the way to the end where an enormous arched window looked out on the now darkening sky.

Their bedroom was large, with polished parquet flooring, an antique looking Persian rug covering most of it. Two huge windows with their ivory shutters open, were either side of a marble fireplace, and a huge wooden sleigh bed stood in the middle of the room. A crystal chandelier hung from the ceiling above the elegantly dressed bed, a dove grey velvet bedcover covering it and matching plump cushions in front of the pillows. A door off the bedroom led into an en-suite bathroom, with marble tiled flooring, a roll top bath and waterfall shower.

Towels and toiletries were laid out by the 'his and hers' marble sinks.

"This is fabulous!" Rebecca said with delight.

"Yes, Declan likes his guests to have everything they could possibly need to feel comfortable, even if they didn't know they needed it! He and Christobel knew a thing or two about creature comforts." Shaun said.

"What was she like? I mean, she was obviously very beautiful..." Rebecca asked, thinking of the lovely looking woman in the photos.

"She was, but she was also charming, and kind. And so well read. She was a skilled conversationalist. He misses her so terribly much." Shaun said as he pulled Rebecca to him.

"And I have found all of those qualities, in you." He kissed her, gently.

They made their way downstairs just before 7pm. Rebecca had changed into the cream silk blouse she'd worn to the ballet, a black leather skirt, and the leopard court shoes. Declan stood to greet them as they entered the library. "You look lovely, my dear." he said. "How is your room?"

"It's perfect, thank you, Declan." Rebecca said.

He poured them aperitifs, and the wolfhounds, now awake, sniffed around them curiously. They came up as high as Rebecca's waist, their heads held on one side as they looked at the visitors inquisitively.

"Don't be afraid, they are very easy-going." Declan smiled, as Rebecca stroked each dog's head, nervously. "They are an introverted breed, believe it or not, very reserved. They are my best friends." he continued, as Kitty appeared at the door, to say she was about to serve dinner.

Declan showed them to the dining room. This also had wooden parquet flooring, partly covered by antique rugs. They sat down at a large round dining table, stylishly laid with a white embroidered tablecloth and heavy silver cutlery, candles alight in crystal candlesticks in the middle. A simple vase of bright orange marigolds was placed between the candles. The fire was lit, a warm glow coming from its embers. Kitty poured their wine into crystal goblets, as Rebecca placed a crisp white linen napkin on her lap.

"Would you like me to serve you, Ma'm?" she asked.

"Oh, thank you." Rebecca, unsure quite what etiquette was required, lifted her plate up. Kitty took it from her, and lifting the lid off a silver tureen, placed new potatoes on it, and then from another tureen, minted lamb chops. She added fine green beans from a cut- glass bowl and placed Rebecca's plate back down.

"Thank you... it looks delicious." she remarked, as Declan smiled. "I have a rather wonderful cook, affectionately known as Ma... Mary. She's been with us a long time, as has Kitty, here." he said.

"The flowers are so pretty, I love marigolds." Rebecca gestured towards them, "My Mother's favourite."

"From my garden, Christobel also loved them. Did you know, they symbolize fierce love, passion and creativity?" Declan smiled across the table at Rebecca as she shook her head.

As they ate, Shaun told Declan how the house was coming along, and about their plans to move in during November.

"And how did you meet this young entrepreneur, Rebecca? One of our very finest…" Rebecca raised an eyebrow.

"Finest?" she asked. Shaun leaned back in his chair as Declan carried on.

"Well, this young man here is Ireland's most successful architect, in fact, architect of the year! Did he not tell you?"

"No, he kept that very quiet, but I can't say I'm surprised. The house at Lough Rosslaire is extraordinary. And Shaun's architectural knowledge when we were in Paris was so… educational." Rebecca looked across at Shaun, feeling somewhat embarrassed that he hadn't told her this. After dinner, they had Irish coffees in the library, and as Declan tended the fire Rebecca stared into the flames, deep in thought. Shaun reached for her hand, stroking her fingers.

"Are you ok, darling?" he asked, concerned.

"Yes, I'm just tired, I might leave you and Declan to it, actually." She said, as she stood up. She thanked Declan for the evening and made her way up to their bedroom. Kitty had been in, as someone had switched the bedside lamps on, and turned the bedcover down. Rebecca sighed and undressed. She went into the en-suite and ran herself a bath.

As she lay back in the hot, scented water, her hair coiled on top of her head, she couldn't stop the nagging doubts that had crept into her head since Declan's revelation. Why would someone as dynamic and famous as

Shaun be interested in her, a married woman of 40 with two grown up kids! He could have anybody, he must have plenty of propositions. She remembered the pretty flight attendant on the first flight, who had flirted with him, and then Vanya, at Buncragga. The waitress at the pub. And then there was the ex, Renee. Was it really over between them? She dried herself and applied body lotion, then put on the new silk pyjamas she had bought, cleaned her teeth, and climbed into the luxurious bed. Curling up on her side, she fell into an uneasy sleep.

She woke with a start, not sure where she was. It was still dark, but she could just make out Shaun, asleep next to her, his breathing soft and shallow. As she turned over, he reached for her, pulling her into him. She lay in his arms like that until morning's light peeped through the shutters. He stroked her head, gently. "How are you, beautiful?" he asked.

"Don't, Shaun." she said, as she pulled herself away from him, sitting up on the edge of the bed. He sat up, reaching for her, as the sheet fell away from him, exposing his tanned, lean torso.

"What is it, Rebecca? What's wrong?" he asked.

"You should have told me!" she said. "I feel foolish, that I didn't know who you really are, you're quite a celebrity here!" she said, tears appearing in her eyes.

"Oh darling, it's not that big a deal! I wanted you to love me for me, not some title I've got! I would have mentioned it, but it didn't seem that important?" he said, pulling her back towards him. She lay back, looking at him. "It *is* important... *you're* important, and me not even knowing that makes me look stupid, don't you see?" she cried.

He held her tightly, as he murmured, "I'm sorry, darling. I didn't think you would feel like that. I'm just not the type to go around telling people who I am or what I've achieved, it's not my style, and meeting you, it's been so refreshing. Your naivety and beauty had me hooked, right from the start. It didn't occur to me I needed to tell you, right away?"

He lowered his head, kissing her lightly, as he whispered sorry, again. Despite her anguish, she responded, kissing him back passionately as he undid the buttons on the silk top, sliding it off her shoulders. He reached for the pyjama shorts, easing them off her gently. He moved slowly down her body, kissing every part of her as she moaned, softly. Lying back, he pulled her on top of him, her legs astride him, and as she lowered herself onto him, he grabbed hold of her hips, moving her rhythmically back and forth on himself, as she closed her eyes and came quietly on him. Then he rolled onto her, and thrust forcefully until he too came inside her, as she wrapped her legs tightly around him.

"It's only you, Rebecca. I don't ever want or need anyone else. Never doubt that, darling." He whispered, as they lay back in the bed. He looked at her intently, and she reached to stroke his chiselled jaw.

"So, how famous? Paparazzi and all that?" She asked.

"No, none of that, Rebecca." He looked serious. "Just the odd tv interview, public appearances, launches. But I've told my agent, once I have settled back here, harassment is off the agenda. It's all forms part of my decision to come back here, to live."

They went down to the dining room, where Kitty had laid out breakfast for them. A tempting spread of fresh fruit salad, yoghurt, pastries and cereal lay before them, with a flask of hot coffee and fresh fruit juice to drink. There was no sign of Declan. They helped themselves and sat down at the round dining table. The sunlight streamed through the tall windows, and Rebecca looked out at the beautiful gardens, an autumnal glow adding a golden tinge across the trees.

"As it's such a lovely day, would you like to see the castle?" Shaun asked. "It's walking distance from here..."

"Yes, I'd love to. And the walk would be good, too." Rebecca answered, as she tucked into a delicious, freshly baked croissant.

Setting off after breakfast, Rebecca wore her new wellingtons and wrapped up warm, as there was a chill in the air, despite the sunshine. Shaun held her hand tightly as they walked down the long drive to the main road.

"So, tell me about the castle?" she asked.

"Parts date to the 12th century, and it's a pretty vast estate, around 260 acres. It's in a regional park, called Demesne. Originally, it was owned by a British knight, Talbot, who escorted Henry II to Ireland, and it remained in the family for nearly 800 years, apart from when Cromwell took it over after the conquest of Ireland. After his demise, they handed it back to the Talbots. It's now owned by the Irish state, but they sold most of its contents, which caused great controversy. There you are... history lesson over!" Shaun laughed.

They walked along the Malahide road, all Rebecca's feelings of insecurity now forgotten about, as they held hands, chatting and enjoying the sun on their faces. Soon, they reached a long, winding driveway which led into beautiful parkland, the turrets of the castle just visible amongst the hundreds of oak trees in the park. Shaun paid the entrance fee at the ticket booth, and they waited for the next escorted tour to begin.

After the tour of the castle, they went to the famous Talbot Botanic gardens behind the castle. There was an enormous walled garden with seven glasshouses and a Victorian conservatory in it, filled with exotic plants, huge ferns, palms, bottlebrushes and many others.

"I love this, it reminds me of the Glass house at Kew!" Rebecca said.

"Yes, it is similar in its construction. According to local history, these plants were brought here by the 7th Talbot of Malahide, mostly from Chile and Australia. He was passionate about collecting rare, exotic species and seeing if they could be grown here. I like the idea of these kinds of plants, they can be so architecturally pleasing. I'd like to do something like this at the house, eventually. What do you think?" He asked, as he took some pictures on his phone.

"I love that idea!" She said, as he turned his phone to her and took a shot.

As lunchtime approached, they left the park and headed back to Declan's house. Shaun suggested going to look at furniture for the house that afternoon.

"Yes, do you have somewhere in mind?" she asked.

"I do, there's a shop in town called Minima. Helen, a lady I met on a couple of projects runs it, and I told her I would come in to see her. It's all quite contemporary, but it combines that really cleverly with art and antiques, so it gives you the vision to create completely unique spaces. It's exactly how I envisage furnishing the place. Do you remember the lights you saw in the house? I chose them from there."

"Yes, I do, they're stunning. I saw something very similar in John Lewis." Rebecca said.

"Tom Dixon designed them. Helen does a lot of his lighting. You'll love the shop, it's right on the quayside, we could get lunch there first?" Shaun suggested.

"Ok, I'll just quickly change." Rebecca said as they arrived back at the house.

"I'll text Helen, tell her we are coming in this afternoon."

They caught a bus into town, which took them to the Quays. Famous for its two roadways and quays running along the north and south banks of the river Liffey, there were seventeen bridges in between. Shaun pointed out major landmarks, such as The Custom

House on Custom-House Quay, and the Four Courts on Inns Quay, home to the Supreme Court of Ireland and the High Court. He told her about the architect who had designed the famous buildings, James Gandon, who had originally entered an architectural competition to design the Royal Exchange in Dublin, in which he came second. Noticed by politicians who were overseeing the redevelopment of Dublin, they chose him for the project, after seeing his clever interpretation of Palladian and Neoclassical building design.

"There was an uproar at the redevelopment, though. Archaeologists had discovered Viking artefacts, many at Wood Quay, where the Vikings had first settled when they arrived here. Actually, there's so much to see at the National Museum, but we'll have to save that for another time, hey?" Shaun told her. "Yes, that would be great to visit." Rebecca replied, realising how little she actually knew about Irish history, considering her Mother was from here!

As they walked along the pavement by the river, Shaun suggested lunch at the famous Quays pub in the Temple Bar area, which he told her was worth seeing for its well- preserved medieval street pattern, comprising lots of little cobbled streets. They walked towards the red brick building that was the pub, as he told her more about the history of 'Dublin's cultural quarter.'

They had a delicious lunch of freshly caught battered cod and home- made fries in the quirky pub, which was surprisingly busy for the time of day. After they had eaten, they headed to the furniture shop, which was on the waterfront at Hanover Quay, the area known as the Grand Canal Basin.

They crossed the busy street towards Minima and went in through the large glass doors. There was a quiet, cool

ambience to the enormous store, with its furniture tastefully displayed. Muted colours, interrupted with vibrant flashes of colour here and there, caught Rebecca's eye, from cushions to rugs, vases to lamp bases. An attractive woman walked over to them, holding her hand out.
"Shaun, it's grand to see you again! It's been a while!" she said, as Shaun reached for her hand and kissed her on each cheek. "It has, Helen. Please meet Rebecca, my fiancée." he stepped aside, as Rebecca extended her hand to Helen.

"Do come into the office, would you like coffee... tea?" she said, as she walked towards the rear of the store, beckoning them to follow. They sat in comfortable white leather chairs in Helen's office, looking at the amazing view over the river, as she ordered tea for them all. Helen sat on the edge of a large oak desk, casually asking how she could help.

"Well, I've finished the house, so we're after furnishing it." Shaun explained, as he showed Helen pictures of it on his phone. As she scrolled through them enthusiastically, she suggested various things for each room. Rebecca could see she had a particular vision for interiors, as she spoke. Their tea arrived, and she handed Shaun's phone back to him.

"Well, you must be over the moon, the house is fabulous!" she exclaimed. "Why don't we have our tea, and then I'll take you through to the showroom, have a look at some ideas?" she suggested, hastily scribbling some notes in a red leather notebook. "Remind me what sort of budget we are looking at, Shaun?"

"Great, Helen. I've also got a few notes, some ideas I've had, along the way. If Rebecca approves what we come up with, we're good to go? The budget is as we talked about before, when I ordered the lighting." Shaun said, reaching into his jacket pocket and retrieving from it the leather journal Rebecca had first noticed at the airport. "Ah, ok. I'll get that pulled up on the I-pad." she said, as she walked round to the other side of the desk to get it.

They looked at the couches first, trying out a few with chaise longue options, reclining features, both fabrics and leathers. Helen suggested they tried the B&B Italia 'Richard' cream leather corner couch, a contemporary module sofa with a classical influence. She showed them on the I-pad the many ways in which the modules of the sofa could fit together, cleverly adapting to preference and room size. As she left them to try it out, they sat on the sumptuous leather, Rebecca trying out the recline option, as Shaun asked her what she thought.

"It's utterly fabulous. I can just envisage it in the living room, around the fire pit, but do you think cream is wise?

Maybe mink, or dove grey?" she suggested, looking at the swatch booklet. "Mind you, I so love this colour. And we could have fur throws over it, to protect it?"

"I like it, a lot. There's a fair bit of grey in the house already, with the slate, the fire pit, and the kitchen units, don't you think?" Shaun asked. Rebecca agreed, and so they decided on that very couch, as Helen worked out the size and configuration of the seating. She suggested two 'Beverly' lounge chairs in a contrasting colour to complement it, they chose these in an oyster grey leather, and two 'Gubi' Epic coffee tables. These were sculptural pieces inspired by Greek columns and Roman architecture, made in Italy from travertine stone in the colour of their choice, so they chose the Vibrant Grey.

They also picked out a console table for the hallway, by B&B Italia. Helen cleverly showed them on the I-pad how their choices would work together, then left them alone while she went to check on availability and delivery of the items.

They wandered over to look at the storage options, liking and then deciding on the 'Rimadesio' Self, which was a modular system to create sideboards, cabinets or wall suspensions. They waited for Helen to return to discuss their endless options on this choice.

"Such a cool shop, I love everything in it!" Rebecca said, and then went on "but I want to contribute, Shaun. When we've sold the house in England, I will have money coming to me."

Shaun placed his fingers to her lips. "Shh. I was coming here anyway. This is where I was going to buy furniture for the place, all along. The fact that you are here choosing it with me, is magic." He smiled lovingly at her, and she felt her heart flutter in her chest. She felt exhausted, deciding on furniture was no simple task. Today had been fun, and interesting, but now she was ready to get back to Declan's house and put her feet up for a bit.

"Tired, darling? Shall we arrange with Helen to come back and look at bedroom and dining furniture tomorrow?" He asked, noticing she was flagging.

"I think so. She should have brochures we can take away to look at tonight?" Rebecca suggested.

Helen came back over to them with the lead times on the sofa, side tables and storage, which were all available within 2 weeks.

"Thanks, Helen. We'd like to come back, maybe tomorrow, to look at bedroom and dining furniture... do you have catalogues?" Shaun asked.

"I'll grab you some, and I'll be here tomorrow from 2pm. Shall we wait until you've finished, then place one order altogether?" she asked.

"Yes, all ordered at the same time would be best. We'll be back tomorrow then. Thanks for your advice today." He said, as he took Rebecca's hand.

"Ah, no problem Lovely to see you again... and to meet you, Rebecca."

It was dusk, as they headed along the waterfront to the bus stop. The Liffey glittered with reflections of the streetlights and the brightly lit apartments that overlooked its banks. The roads were quieter now, rush hour was long over. Shaun held her hand, the brochures tucked under his other arm.

"I can visualize that couch, and the side tables, in the living area. I think we chose well. I'll work out the shelving and storage when we move in." Shaun said, sounding pleased.

"Me too. I think they will complement it perfectly. I can't wait to see how it all looks!" Rebecca said, excitedly. He squeezed her hand as the bus to Malahide pulled into the stop.

Declan had also just arrived back at the house as they walked up the long drive.

"Hello, you two. How are you? Join me for tea in the library?" he asked, smiling.

"We'd love to, thank you." said Rebecca, as they followed him in through the front door, and into the library. The fire had been lit, and the room felt warm and inviting, as Duke and Duchess jumped up from the hearth to greet them. Kitty arrived with the tea, placing it on the table beside the chesterfield. She poured it into delicate china cups for them, handing Rebecca one first, then the men. Declan asked them about their day, and Rebecca said how much she'd enjoyed seeing the castle. Shaun went on to tell him about the furniture expedition.

"Ah, yes, Minima. They have some fine furniture. What did you choose?" he asked, interested. Shaun showed him pictures, and he nodded, approvingly.

"We're not done yet, though. We were both shopped out, so we 're going back there tomorrow to look at bedroom and dining pieces." Shaun said. Declan told them about the furniture his old friend and onetime colleague, Warren Platner, had designed. He was famous for designing the interior of the 'Windows on the World' restaurant in the World Trade Centre, and the Georg Jensen Design Centre, prior to turning his hand to furniture for Knoll.

"I believe they sell some of his designs in Minima." he told them, "though he sadly passed away in 2006. Still, brilliant design never dies." he said, sadly.

"Terribly sad he would have seen the destruction of the World Trade Centre towers, with all those poor people losing their lives in it." Rebecca said.

"Indeed, that was an abhorrence of evil." Declan said.

After tea, they went up to relax and change before dinner. Rebecca sat on one of the velvet boudoir chairs, undoing her trainers. Sitting opposite her on a matching footstool, Shaun took one of her feet in his hands, massaging it gently.

"How long will we stay, Shaun? Have you arranged anything?" she asked, looking worried. "I don't want to outstay our welcome, that's all."

"It disappointed him when I said a few days to him, said we should stay for longer! He's quite lonely, now, without Christobel." Shaun replied.

"How old is he? Does he still work?" she asked. Shaun said he was seventy-two and still working on a private consultation basis. "He's still very sought after, but he took a step back from it all when his wife died. I don't think he will ever get over her."

"No children?" Rebecca asked.

"No, just the dogs. They are like children, to him." Shaun said, as he took her other foot and rubbed that one, soothingly.

"That feels good..." She sighed, as she leant her head back against the chair, closing her eyes.

"Shall I run you a bath?" He suggested.

"No, I think I'll wait until after dinner, or I won't feel like getting dressed up again. I'll just freshen up, I think." She replied, stretching her arms out.

"Ok darling, I'll do the same, shall I go first?"

She brushed her hair and touched up her makeup, changing into her cream blouse and leather jeans, with the leopard heels.

"You look lovely, darling." Shaun said as he pulled her into his arms. "I'm glad I bought these shoes, I can reach you better!" she laughed, as she kissed him.

"I'd like to see you in just those shoes…" he murmured, his voice husky.

Kitty served dinner at 7pm, as before. Tonight, 'Ma' had made a Shepherd's pie, served with tender stem broccoli. It was a delicious, comforting dinner, followed by a rhubarb fool for dessert. As Kitty cleared away, Rebecca thanked Declan for his hospitality, and said she hoped they weren't a burden, a thought that was weighing heavily on her mind.

Refilling her wineglass with a velvety malbec, he said genuinely, "It's a joy to have your company. Shaun is like a son to me, which means you will become like my daughter-in-law."

"Thank you, Declan." she said, blushing. She wondered how much Shaun had told him about her past, which seemed so sordid to her, now.

After Irish coffees and brandy in the library, they said their goodnights and went up to bed. Shaun ran a bath for Rebecca while she undressed and removed her makeup. She stepped into the luxurious foaming water which was just the right temperature and laid back, taking a small crystal glass of brandy from him, which he'd poured from a decanter on the dressing table.

"It's like staying in a hotel!" She smiled, taking a sip of the delicious amber liquid.

"Are you sure you're up for going back to Minima tomorrow?" He asked. "I've had a look through the brochures, and I've seen what I like, shall I show you?" he said.

"Oh, do. After a good night's sleep, I shall be really up for it!"

He brought the catalogue in, showing her a photo of a four-poster bed, a classic canopy style with wooden posts. It was a minimalist, modern interpretation. "It sits on a platform, with storage underneath, and the headboard can be leather or fabric. What do you think? I like the fact we can position it mid room, like the picture."

"It's stunning... but we need to see it. Do they have it in the showroom?" Rebecca asked.

"I can text Helen and find out, but look at this, too." He showed her the 'Gubi' Epic dining table, which was the same neutral travertine as the side tables they'd chosen earlier, shown with 'Gubi' Bat chairs, upholstered in a fabric of their choice but in the picture they were shown in green velvet.

"Ooh, gorgeous! I love them, I am looking forward to going and looking again, now!" she said, as he put the brochure down and leaned over the side of the bath to kiss her.

They got in to bed and slept, entwined in each other's arms. As dawn broke, Rebecca felt Shaun's fingers gently stroking her back, hips, thighs and then round to her breasts, as she felt him harden against her. Turning into him, he pulled her towards him, straddling her and kissing her deeply as he entered her.

She arched her back and threw her head back wantonly, and as his pace quickened, she raised her hips, her arms around him as she pulled him in deeper. "God, I love you so much," he gasped as he shuddered into her, his eyes blazing in the dim morning light. She pulled him down onto her, and they lay, just like that, for some minutes, his breath rasping against her neck.

After a leisurely breakfast, taken with Declan on the terrace as it was a beautiful, sunny morning, they set off for town. Shaun wanted to show Rebecca all that Grafton street, most famous for its buskers, offered. Telling her how it had been the musical heart of Dublin in the 1980s, they walked along it towards the busy thoroughfare through St. Stephen's Green.

They passed the equally famous 47acre site of Trinity College where Shaun told her he would have studied Civil and Structural Engineering until going to a careers evening.

An architect was speaking at the event, and Shaun had realised that this was his true vocation, instead. It devastated his mother, his leaving Ireland for Paris, then London, when the time came. Rebecca admired the beautiful Georgian buildings that the college was famous for, and as they walked past it, she wondered how differently things might have turned out, had Shaun gone there.

Helen greeted them as they walked in to 'Minima.'

"How are you today?" she smiled, extending her hand.

"Much better prepared!" Shaun laughed as he took her hand. "We'd like to see the 'Gubi' Epic dining table, barstools and look at some chairs, then on to bedroom furniture."

"Ok, well, follow me." She said, leading them to another part of the showroom. The table was on display with the green velvet chairs, but Helen said she had some other chairs she wanted them to see. She took them over to see the 'Edra' Ella chairs, and Rebecca gasped when she saw them. Pedestal dining chairs in the shape of a flower, with the seatbacks being almost transparent, in soft hues of green and blue.

"With your views of the ocean one side, the mountains the other, I think these would be perfect for your dining area." Helen said, smiling as though she'd hit the jackpot.

"They are stunning, aren't they, Rebecca?" Shaun said, as he tried one out. "Polycarbonate, are they?" He asked.

"Entirely, God, they'd last you a lifetime!" Helen said. "And, if you 'd like a rug for the area, I have the perfect one!"

"Let's have a look, then." Shaun said, getting up from the chair and letting Rebecca try it out. Helen led them to the rugs, pulling out an ombre wool rug from its hanger, in varying shades of green.

"This is by 'CC Tapis,' it's called the 'Dusk' rug, handmade in Nepal." Shaun and Rebecca reached to touch it, and both agreed it was perfect to go with the chairs.

"Well, that wasn't difficult, Helen. Have I blown the budget yet?" Shaun said, laughing.

"You have not, and we'll be offering you a good discount for your custom!" She laughed, winking at him. Next, they looked at the 'Gubi' Beetle barstools the inspiration of which, Helen elaborated, came from the 'insect' world. The designer GamFratesi had carefully studied the anatomy, aesthetics and movement of a beetle, with the resulting design reinterpreting characteristics of a beetle's different sections; its shape, shell, hard exterior and soft insides. Four of these barstools were chosen, in a greenish blue polycarbonate which complemented the dining chairs perfectly.

Then they went upstairs to look at the bedroom furniture, where Helen showed them the bed that Shaun had texted her about.

"So, here it is, it's by 'Maxalto,' the 'Alcova' bed." They had a good look at it, lay on it, admired it, but weren't that sure, after all. Rebecca said she'd like to see something a little more sleek, glamorous, even. Helen took them over and showed them the B&B Italia 'Richard' bed.

"This has the same lines as the sofa, see." She showed them the beautiful King size dove grey fabric bed, with its mattress and headboard raised high above the lateral bed sides. Shaun loved it for its architecturally clean lines, Rebecca for its height, so they decided on that one, together with a Hypnos sprung mattress and two elegant B&B Italia 'Awa' bedside tables, made from a material called 'Cristalplant' which was soft to touch, with a white, glossy finish. Helen left them while she went to complete the calculations and delivery date, as Rebecca lay back on the show bed they'd chosen.

"Yes, this will be perfect." she said, imagining the bed in situ, with the far-reaching views beyond. She realised she actually couldn't wait to be in the house now, to get settled in and be in one place, home...

Shaun smiled as he kissed the tip of her nose. "Aye, it's all coming together. I think we've chosen well... a good joint effort!" he said, as he sat on the edge of the bed beside her.

It was almost dark when they left the showroom, all the paperwork done and duplicated for them to take away in a thick cream wallet. It was drizzling, so they took shelter and waited for the bus. When they got back to Declan's house, Kitty let them in and told them Declan was in the library waiting for them, when they were ready to join him.

They freshened up and changed, then went downstairs for pre-dinner drinks.

"Ah, welcome! How was your day, today?" Declan said, standing up to greet them.

"Great, we chose most of the furniture for the house. Helen is good, she has vision, as does Rebecca." Shaun said, reaching for the gin & tonics Declan had prepared for them. He handed one to Rebecca as she sat down, stroking each dog as she did so. They moved closer to her, resting their heavy heads against her knees. She'd grown fond of them, surprisingly, never really having been that interested in dogs before. Taking a sip from the ice-cold drink, she relaxed back into the sofa, as Shaun sat down beside her, and Declan stoked the fire.

"I shall look forward to seeing the place. Do you have an actual moving in date, yet?" he asked, as he took a seat opposite them.

"It's looking like mid- November, maybe a bit before. We'll be staying at Bridie's cottage at the port, till then." Shaun replied, as he put his hand on Rebecca's knee, lightly.

"And how do you feel about moving here, Rebecca?" Declan asked her.

"Well, I'm no stranger to Ireland, though I've seen more of Dublin this time than ever before. My mother is from Donegal, and we used to visit her sister there every summer, when I was a child. I used to so enjoy those trips." Rebecca explained.

"Ah, so you're coming home?" He laughed, winking at her.

"Yes, I suppose I am." She said smiling, as she finished her drink.

Dinner was served, tonight's meal a delicious lobster Thermidor, freshly caught and prepared, Declan told them, proudly. Accompanied by a crisp green salad, Rebecca savoured every mouthful of her favourite dish, as Declan refilled her glass with a delightful dry white wine. As they ate, Declan asked her more about her background.

"I lived in London… Richmond, with my ex-husband. I've two grown-up sons, James and Sam." She said, faltering slightly.

"And grand lads they are, too." Shaun interjected.

"I'm sure they take after you, my dear." He said, smiling warmly at her. She felt relieved that the revelation was out. But really, she'd had nothing to worry about, she realised. Declan was utterly charming, and so kind to her.

"Well, Shaun is, as I told you, like a son to me. Anything I can ever do to help you both, you must not hesitate to ask." He said, as they finished the main course and Kitty appeared to clear their plates.

Back in the room, Shaun ran a bath as Rebecca undressed. She slipped into the water as he took his clothes off and joined her, sitting behind her with his legs wrapped around her.

He gently kneaded her shoulders as she sighed, relaxing back into him.

"Are you ok, darling?" he asked.

"Yes, I really am. It's been nice, staying here, meeting Declan." she said.

"Good, I'm glad you feel like that. Last day tomorrow, then we'll head off late morning Saturday, pick up a hire car from the airport. How does that sound?" he whispered, as he nuzzled her neck.

"That's fine. What shall we do tomorrow, head into town again?" she replied, as she leant her head to one side.

"Yes, we can go to Brown Thomas. It's Dublin's answer to Selfridges. We need some things for the house." he said, as he stepped out of the bath and wrapped a towel round his waist. She stood up, and he handed her the robe that was hanging on the back of the door.

"Ok, but I'm picking up the bill for everything, alright?" Rebecca said firmly, as she smiled and put a robe on. After brushing her teeth and applying her night cream, she climbed into the freshly made bed next to him, her head falling back on the soft pillows. She felt his lips on her, his tongue moving slowly all over her, tingling from the minty toothpaste. She arched her back as he moved down her body, kissing and licking her intimately, and before long she felt herself coming, as he grabbed her bottom, pulling her closer into his mouth.

The next morning was beautiful. Kitty served breakfast on the terrace, as the wolfhounds stretched out languidly in the sunshine. "What are you two up to, today?" Declan asked, as he helped himself to the crispy bacon and grilled tomatoes Kitty had placed on the table.

"We're heading into town again, we've a few more things to get for the house." Shaun replied, as he put some food on Rebecca's plate.

"Well, I'll be in town myself, I could meet you for a late lunch?" Declan said.

"That would be lovely, Declan. My treat." Rebecca said, as she tucked into the delicious breakfast.

They arranged to meet at Hugh Brown's restaurant, in Brown Thomas, which Declan highly recommended, at 2pm.

The bus stopped on Clarendon street, near to the famous department store, where uniformed doormen greeted customers. As they walked through the double doors into the store, one of the doormen holding the door open said, "Good morning, Mr. Forsythe, good morning, Madam." Rebecca looked at Shaun as he shrugged, smiling.

"I suppose I shall have to get used to this!" She said, as they made their way into the huge, high-ceilinged perfume hall towards the elevators.

They looked at kitchenware first, choosing a Le Creuset cast iron cookware set in artic white, with matching salt and pepper grinders, and a Le Creuset stainless steel pan set. Royal Doulton's 'Bowl of Plenty' dinnerware set in a grey and white glaze to complement the kitchen units. Kitchen tools by Stellar and Alessi, a de Longhi toaster, Robert Welch cutlery. Rebecca checked off the list they'd made as they added things to their trolley.

While they made their way around the store looking at all the lovely creative displays, Rebecca couldn't help noticing people, women particularly, openly staring at Shaun, who seemed oblivious to it. Well, she thought, let them. He was with her, in love with her. She brushed off the insecurities that seemed to cloud her happiness.

"I could do with a coffee, darling?" Shaun said, pushing the now full trolley.

"Yes, me too, where shall we leave this?" she asked, looking around.

"We'll take it over to the counter, they can keep it by. I think we'll get it all delivered anyway, easier than carting it all back to Declan's."

The café was busy, but they found a table and Shaun went to order the coffees. They sat and drank them, looking at the home furnishings/bedding catalogue they'd picked up on the way in.

"Silk or linen?" Rebecca asked, looking at Shaun furtively.

"Silk… every time." He looked at her, his eyes glinting wickedly.

"We must get a washer/drier with a special setting, so I don't ruin them!" she laughed.

"We can get all the electrical stuff in Donegal, there's a pretty good place there." he said, looking at his watch. "We've an hour till we meet Declan, shall we go look at this bedding?"

They retrieved their trolley and went up to the next level, where they found some gorgeous 'GingerLily' silk bedding in silver and 'Nimbus' duvets and pillows. Then, they chose 'Christy' towels and bathmats in a soft mink colour, and went to a pay point. Rebecca insisted on paying for everything, much to Shaun's disapproval. Arranging delivery of all the items for the beginning of November, Shaun gave the sales assistant the address of the house, and then they made their way up to the next floor, where they saw Declan waiting for them outside the stylish, newly refurbished 'Hugh Brown's.'

They were shown to a booth, and Shaun helped Rebecca with her jacket. As they sat down, Declan suggested champagne. "Why not, it is past 12?" Shaun laughed. Rebecca agreed, she felt like she needed one with what she'd spent. Still, she would have enough to get by, once they sold the house, she thought to herself.

The menu was mouth- watering. Rebecca chose smoked salmon with a pink fir potato salad, Declan the same, and Shaun ordered a chicken Caesar salad.. The champagne arrived in chilled flutes, and as they toasted a successful shopping trip, Declan handed Rebecca an envelope.

"I'd like to get you something for the new house, whatever you like, so please accept this."

"Oh Declan, you shouldn't have!" Rebecca exclaimed, as she opened the envelope and saw a 350.00 Euro gift card for Brown Thomas. She handed it to Shaun to see.

As Shaun looked at the card, he chastised Declan. "It's too much, fella! There's no need, you coming and visiting us and staying a bit is enough!"

"Ah, nonsense. You buy yourselves something lovely for the house, then you can remember me by it!" he said, as their lunch arrived.

The food was delicious, and as Rebecca made her way to the ladies' room, she asked the waiter to bring the bill straight to her, when she was back at the table. She washed her hands, looking at herself in the smoked glass mirror, and saw the champagne had given her skin a glow. Smiling at her reflection, she applied a nude gloss to her full, rosy lips.

Rebecca paid for the lunch, though both men tried to intervene. "No, I absolutely insist." She said assertively, handing the waiter her card. Finishing up their champagne, they left the restaurant. Declan went off to let them finish shopping, and deciding to look at mirrors, they ended up choosing a huge, art deco style square mirror, which they thought would look good in the entrance hall of the house, above the console table. Paying for it with Declan's gift card, they added that to the delivery already arranged, and then headed down to the enormous food hall for a last look.

Rebecca purchased exotic curry powders, spices and oils, tea towels, aprons and oven gloves, and then, deciding they'd had enough, left the amazing store.

"I'm exhausted!" Rebecca said, as they strolled to the bus stop. Shaun rubbed her shoulders and pulled her into him.

"Well, we've done alright. I'm really pleased with what we've chosen." He said.

"Me too, I just can't wait to be in the house, now!" She replied, as the bus pulled into their stop.

Back at Declan's, Kitty brought tea into the library, and they sat by the fire Declan had prepared, as the daylight faded. Rebecca showed Declan a picture of the mirror they'd chosen with his generous gift.

"That's lovely. Where will it go?" he asked.

"Above a console table, in the hall, we think." Rebecca replied.

"But not opposite the front door... no negative Feng Shui!" Shaun laughed. Rebecca looked at him, surprised.

"I wouldn't have expected that from you! But then I guess it's so important, in architecture?" She said.

"Indeed, it is." Declan said. "Interestingly, many clients won't work with architects who haven't at least partly studied Feng Shui's Chinese traditions, it's become fashionable and in-demand, especially in Western interior design and architecture."

Rebecca looked across at Shaun teasingly; "You must fill me in on the special traditions you followed in the house?"

"That I will." He replied, as he winked at her.

The next morning, they packed up their belongings and carried them down to the hallway. Shaun had booked a taxi to the airport for an hour's time, so they joined Declan in the dining room for breakfast.

When they'd finished the hearty spread Ma had made for them, Rebecca thanked him for his hospitality, and made him promise he would visit them when they were settled.

The taxi arrived, and Declan hugged Rebecca, kissing her on both cheeks.

"It has been delightful meeting you, my dear. I know you will make this lad a terrific wife." He said, as she felt her cheeks becoming flushed. He shook Shaun's hand vigorously as the taxi pulled up outside.

As they pulled away, they waved goodbye and Rebecca suddenly felt sad for him, all alone, waving to them from the doorstep.

Chapter 15.

Donegal.

Shaun drove out of the airport in the comfortable 4x4 they'd hired, heading for the N3 out of Dublin. It was a bright morning, the roads fairly clear, as it was a Saturday.

"It'll take us about three hours" he said, as he reached over and squeezed her hand. "You ok?" He asked.

"I'm okay. I felt sad leaving Declan, though. Isn't that strange? I've only known him a few days!" She replied.

"Aye, well, he's a rare breed, is Declan. A very special man." Shaun reflected.

Through undulating green hills and craggy mountains, before long they were near Sligo on the N4, its famous 'Ben Bulben' mountain appearing in the distance, after a couple of hours driving.

"I used to get so excited as a child, seeing this view!" Rebecca said. "Probably because I knew it meant we were nearly at Aunt Norah's. I used to hate the journey!"

"It's much better now, with the new road system. Have you ever walked up there?" Shaun asked.

"No... have you?" She replied.

"Yes... it's a bloody hike! I climbed about 8km in two-and-a-half hours, but it's worth it, the views are stunning out to Mullaghmore and across to Slieve League, all Yeats country, as it's known. We must do it together?" he said.

"Yes, I'd like that." She said, smiling to herself. She'd never have considered climbing a mountain before, ever!

What changes he had brought to her life.

After about three and a half hours, they reached the port where Bridie's cottage was, and Shaun pulled up alongside it.

They got out, stretching their legs, just as the afternoon sun was fading. There was a key left under the mat outside the front door, and as Shaun opened it and they made their way in, Rebecca remembered her first night here, with him. It seemed like such a long time ago, and yet the place felt cosy and familiar, welcoming. There was milk and butter in the fridge, and eggs and bread on the countertop. Shaun came up behind her, wrapping his arms around her as he bent and kissed her neck.

"Welcome back. I bet all the curtains are already twitching!" He said, as she turned round towards him. He kissed her, gently then searchingly, pulling her tight into his arms, as she felt his arousal against her. He grabbed her hand, and they made their way into the bedroom, undressing each other as they went, kicking their shoes off and collapsing onto the bed, as Shaun pulled her jeans off and lowered himself onto her, easing her panties down as he did so.

"I cannot get enough of you, darling!" He whispered, as he bent his head to her breasts.

They lay there, in each other's arms, as darkness fell. He stroked her head, as he said, "I love you so much, my darling." She moved further into him, resting her head on his chest, stroking the dark, silky hair there.

"And this is where it all began." She replied.

"No, it began when I first set eyes on you, Rebecca."

They got up and while she showered, Shaun retrieved their things from the car. She unpacked her bag and changed into her new jeans and pale pink sweater, and while Shaun got ready, she quickly dried her hair and tidied the ruffled bedcover, smiling to herself. They headed out to the 'Rising Tide' pub for dinner, and it felt good to be back at the little port. The stars were just appearing in the velvety sky, and the familiar lights on the moored boats twinkling away.

Locals nodded and greeted them as they made their way into the pub and sat down at a small, round table by the fire. They ordered the home-made lasagne and greens, Shaun had Guinness while Rebecca drank red wine. When the food arrived, they tucked in heartily and talked about their plans for the next few days.

Back at the cottage, Rebecca undressed, brushed her teeth and climbed into the comfortable bed. It was so peaceful. Shaun climbed in beside her, turning off the single lamp by the bed. He kissed her gently, and they fell asleep, entwined, almost immediately.

The sun streaming in through the thin cotton curtains woke them, as Rebecca looked at her phone... it was past nine am. She saw that they'd slept a solid ten hours, and realised she was desperate for the loo, jumping up out of the bed. After splashing her face with cold water to wake herself up, Rebecca put a jumper on over her pyjamas.

It felt chillier than it had recently, she thought, as she went to boil the kettle for tea. Handing Shaun a mug of steaming tea, she sat on the edge of the bed, drinking hers.

"I slept so well! It's so quiet here!" She said.

"It's even quieter out at Lough Rosslaire, I do hope you're going to like it, darling?" He said, raising himself up on one elbow as he stroked her hair.

"Of course I will! I'll be with you!" she said, as she put her tea down and climbed back into bed.

After a hearty breakfast of scrambled eggs and soda bread, which Shaun made while Rebecca took her shower, they headed out for a walk in the bright morning sunshine. When they reached the steps down to the harbour, an old man in a flat cap waved at them.

"Top of the morning, Shaun!" He called out, a gap filled grin widening on his tanned, leathery face.

"Uncle Seamus! Morning! How are you?" Shaun replied, as they walked over to where the old man was working, untangling a pile of old fishing nets.

"This is Rebecca, my wife to be." He said, as Rebecca extended her hand. Seamus took off a battered leather glove and shook her hand.

"Well, aren't you a sight for sore eyes!" he said, shaking her hand vigorously. Rebecca laughed as she shook his hand back.

"This is my mam's brother." Shaun explained.

"Are you back for good, now? Bridget tells me they finished the house?"

"Aye, it's all but finished. We'll be moving in soon. You must come visit." Shaun said.

"That I will, when the salmon have finished spawning. Busy time for me, now!" Seamus sighed.

They said goodbye, and walked on round the road, which looked out across the bay. The sea was sparkling in the sunlight, calm as a millpond.

"Gosh, how old is he?" Rebecca asked.

"Seamus must be seventy… he was the youngest of eight." Shaun said.

"Wow, still fishing?" She replied.

"They never stop! It's in their blood." He laughed.

They walked for an hour, Shaun greeting a few people as they passed. He asked her whether she'd like to meet his sister, Bridget, that afternoon.

"Yes, why not? Is she far from here?" Rebecca said.

"No, it's about a twenty-minute drive, just down the coastal road. You'll get to meet her husband, Liam, if he's there. They have two boys, but I suspect they'll be at work. Niall works in town, for a bank, and Dermot will be out fishing. I'll call her, after lunch." He said, as they headed back to the cottage. They found a small brown paper bag sitting on the doorstep when they got back there. Shaun picked it up and looking inside, it was crammed full of fresh whitebait.

"Do you like them?" He asked, smiling wryly.

"I don't know! Try me! I know Mum and Norah always had them, as kids."

"I'll fry some up, see what you think. You must get used to things being left on doorsteps..."

"I rather like that idea!" She laughed.

Shaun fried the tiny whitebait in some seasoned flour that he found in a cupboard, and some butter. As they crisped, he handed her one to try.

"Mmm, delicious!" She exclaimed. They were so fresh and tasty, perfectly fried.

He piled a plate with the remaining ones and they sat and ate them, with the leftover soda bread, and tea.

"A perfect lunch, thank you!" Rebecca said, as she took the plates to the sink.

"Lemon squeezed over would have been nice... next time, maybe."

"Who do you think left them?" she asked, remembering the daily catch always left at Aunt Norah's door, all those summers ago.

"Oh, anyone just back in on their boat... they would all know we are here!" he laughed, as he dialled Bridget's number on his phone.

They arrived at Bridget's little farmhouse just after 3pm, and she came out to greet them. Older than Shaun by five years, she was an attractive woman, with similar chiselled features to Shaun, and the same piercing blue eyes. Tanned skin and black hair in a loose bun, just a few hints of grey at her temples, Rebecca could see the striking resemblance straightaway.

"Welcome, welcome. It's Rebecca, isn't it?" She said, as she walked over. Taken aback, Rebecca felt Bridget's arms around her, hugging her tightly.

"Yes, pleased to meet you." Rebecca said, as Bridget released her from her grasp, studying her closely. Shaun hugged his sister, chastising her for her scrutiny of Rebecca. "Well, Mammy would approve." she said, nodding. "Come in, come in. Liam has gone to get peat for the fire, he'll be back soon." She said, as they followed her into the whitewashed cottage, avoiding the free-range chickens that were grazing everywhere.

Inside, it was a typical Irish croft cottage, warm and welcoming, but simply furnished. They sat at the kitchen table while Bridget made them tea, and Rebecca looked at the old photos that were on every bit of wall space there was.

Shaun pointed to different pictures of his parents, siblings, himself at various stages of childhood. Most of them were in black and white, a few later ones had progressed to colour.

"It's good to have you home." Bridget said, placing mugs of strong tea down in front of them. "Is it for good, now?" She asked.

"It is, and Rebecca will be here with me. We are engaged, Bridget." Shaun said.

"My Lord, when did that happen? You've been keeping secrets from me!" She said, surprise on her face.

Rebecca spoke up. "Shaun asked me a few weeks ago, when we were in France, visiting my parents." She explained.

"France! But I thought you met here, in Ireland?" Bridget looked confused.

"We did, but then we had to go back to England, and then we visited Rebecca's parents, in France." Shaun explained.

"Hmm, they obviously pay you too much, in that fancy job of yours!" She said, obvious pride on her face.

"Don't believe everything you hear, Brig." He said affectionately, at which point Bridget's husband appeared in the doorway.

"Ah, Shaun! Welcome home!" Liam said, shaking Shaun's hand as he turned to Rebecca.

"This is Shaun's fiancée, Rebecca." Bridget said. Liam shook her hand as Rebecca took in his handsome, rugged features. Tall, and as tanned as Bridget, his hair was completely white, but his stubble dark, and his eyes a bright, cornflower blue.

"Pleasure to meet you, miss." He said, as he put a bucket full of peat down by the fire.

Rebecca glanced at Shaun, guessing he hadn't told them too much about her past. Oh well, it could wait. They drank their tea, chatting about the house and the furniture that was coming, and before long it had grown dark outside.

"We'll head off now, but we will visit soon… maybe when the boys are here?" Shaun stood up and handed Rebecca her jacket. Bridget hugged them both, Liam more formally shaking hands as he said his goodbyes.

Shaun drove back towards the port, as stars appeared in the clear evening sky.

"I really like them… a great couple!" Rebecca said, as Shaun reached for her hand.

"They liked you too... I could tell. Not that that's any surprise." He said, squeezing her fingers tight.

They had dinner at the pub again that evening, freshly caught salmon, served with new potatoes and river samphire, which Rebecca had never tried.

"I like it... it's salty, but it balances out with the lemon on the salmon which is the best I've ever tasted." She commented.

"It will be, never fresher than when caught here." Shaun said as he refilled her wine glass. "So, tomorrow. I've some calls in the morning, but shall we head to town after to look at white goods?" He suggested.

"Sounds like a plan. I'll check all my admin while you make your calls. It's been a few days, I expect they have inundated me with emails!" Rebecca sighed, finishing her wine. They left the pub and walked the short distance back to the cottage, which felt warm and welcoming now the evenings were growing colder.

Next morning, Shaun brought Rebecca a mug of tea and her laptop. The sun was shining brightly through the thin curtains.

"Morning, darling. How did you sleep?" he said, as he leant over and kissed her bare shoulder.

"So well. It's the quiet. I've never known such peace." She said, as she took a sip of tea.

"Yes, this is the solitude I longed for when I was in London. But mine is just about to be invaded for a while, so I'll leave you to it for a bit." He said, handing her laptop to her.

Clicking on her emails, she saw she had 168 unread, and sighed as she propped the pillow behind her and trawled through them. Once she'd deleted all the junk, she saw several from the solicitor which she opened in date order. The first few were just regular updates to advise her matters were proceeding smoothly. The last two, one from a week previously and one dated the day before, were to advise her that the *"Decree Absolut"* would be ready to sign the following week, and a signature request for a financial order, to permit the sale of the marital home.

There were also two from Nigel. She took a deep breath as she clicked on the first.

"Dear Rebecca, I hope you and your new boyfriend are well. As you may now be aware, the house is to be sold, and you will receive half of its worth, once we pay any outstanding fees. I have had three valuations, and the most realistic has come in at £775,000. Let me know if you agree. The market is good, according to the agents I've spoken to.

The solicitor has written, and they will complete the divorce next week. I haven't told the boys; I thought you could do that?

I hope we can meet, amicably, one day. Nigel."

She felt choked as she read the email, and her eyes welled with tears. Poor, pathetic Nigel. Why had she stayed with him? She wiped her nose with a tissue as she opened his second email.

"You bitch. You are a fucking bitch. How could you humiliate me like this? Everyone's talking about how you've gone off with some idiot you've only known 5 minutes! Stupid cow! Think you're going to be happy? You'll never be happy, not if I've got anything to do with it!"

Shaking as she shut the laptop down, she got up and went into the bathroom, and turned the shower to its hottest setting. Stepping into it and letting the water pound her body, she felt scared for the first time since she'd met Shaun. Could it true? Were people really talking about her? Was she a fool for thinking this was the right thing, leaving England to be with Shaun? Would she ever truly be free of Nigel, wherever she was? The water washed away the tears that were falling, uncontrollably. She heard the bathroom door open, and Shaun asking her if she was ok.

"Yes, I'll be out in a minute..." She sobbed, her voice sounding distorted.

"What's wrong?" He asked, sounding concerned.

Turning the shower off, she pulled the curtain aside, and Shaun handed her a towel. She took it, burying her face into it and sobbing. Shaun took her in his arms.

"What is it?" he asked.

He made her another cup of tea as she dried herself and got dressed. She opened up the laptop, clicked on the two emails from Nigel, and handed it to him. As he read them, she saw his jaw harden. He clicked it shut and put it down on the table.

"The guy's an arsehole, Rebecca, you mustn't let him get to you. It's good news, next week you'll be free of the marriage. The financial side of things might take a while yet, but at least you're a free woman… my woman!" He said, as he pulled her to him, stroking her head and breathing in the scent of her.

"I'm scared." She said.

"Why? You've nothing to fear, I will take care of you!" Shaun said, as he held her tight.

"What if he never really let's go? What if he sets out to destroy any happiness I think I have found?" she whispered.

"I won't let him, Rebecca." Shaun replied.

Chapter 16.

The House. (Teach an Tobar.)

Finally, the day had arrived to move into the new house. Delivery of the furniture had been on time the week before, and now the dust sheets placed over it were ready to remove. The electrician who had installed the white goods let them know everything was ready and working, and the heating was on, so the house would be warm when they got there, he told Shaun.

Rebecca could feel her excitement mounting as she made tea for them. It was a bright morning, though bitterly cold. As Shaun showered, she made their last breakfast in the little cottage. She'd already stripped the bed and tidied everything away. Packing all done, she waited for Shaun to come out of the bathroom.

"That smells good! A bacon sandwich... perfect!" He said, as she handed him the plate. As he ate the sandwich, he looked across the table at her.

"You ok, darling?" He asked.

"I'm excited! Nervous, but excited!" She replied.

"Don't be nervous, it's going to be perfect. I know it." He said, as he finished his tea.

They arrived at the house later that morning, as the last few workmen were packing up their tools. Shaun parked and got out to open Rebecca's door for her. They walked up the gravel path, holding hands, as the wind whipped around them and the house stood magnificent and proud before them. Shaun opened the front door, and they stepped inside. The sun shone through all the vast windows, flooding the place with light. Rebecca took her jacket and boots off, and walked in.

"Welcome home." Shaun said, taking her tightly in his arms and kissing her.

While Shaun went out to speak to the workmen before they left, Rebecca stood looking at the panoramic view from the living room. The wide expanse of the ocean stretched out in front of her, as far as the eye could see, until it merged with the horizon and became a hazy blur. There were hundreds of white horses on it today, as the winds were so strong. Perhaps they would take a walk down there later, if it wasn't too cold, she thought to herself.

Walking into the kitchen, she unpacked the box of provisions they had brought to tide them over. She made tea, using the Quooker tap fitted on the central island. How fantastic, she thought, as she watched the tap dispense boiling water, no need for a kettle! As she stirred the tea someone suddenly opened the back door, making her jump.

A workman popped his head in, taking his hard hat off, and said,

"We are off on our way now! Hope you will be very happy here, it's a grand house!"

"Oh! Thank you, it is! I'm sure we will! You've all done an amazing job!" She replied, startled.

Shaun came into the kitchen, his cheeks red and his hair tousled from the wind.

"Ah, tea! Lovely! How's the tap?" he asked, as he took the mug she handed him.
"It's brilliant... boiling hot. I love it."

They unpacked the boxes in the kitchen as they drank their tea. It thrilled Rebecca to see all their lovingly chosen purchases finding their way into their new cupboards and onto shelves. Next, they removed the dust sheets from the furniture. First, they unveiled the dining table and chairs. They sat down and marvelled again at how comfortable the 'Gubi' chairs were.

They positioned the table closer to the rear windows and saw how the chairs did indeed pick out the colours of the high, rugged mountains which were covered now, in thrift and heather.

The couch was next; they placed it at an angle in front of the living room widow and pulled the dust sheet off it. They sat on it, lay on it, kissed on it.

"It's perfect." Rebecca sighed, stretching her arms back behind her head, her eyes closed.

They arranged the side tables and the hall console. The rug Helen had recommended was unrolled, and placed in the dining area, its colours complementing the chairs and views exactly as she had predicted.

Upstairs, they uncovered the beautiful bed they had chosen, which was facing out of the room, looking to the sea beyond. They lay down on it, holding hands and admiring the view.

"Just as I hoped it would be." Shaun said, reaching across to her and pulling her on top of him, as she felt his hardness against her.

"I want you, now." He groaned as he pulled her jumper up over her breasts and leant to kiss each one in turn.

"Let's wait... let's finish unpacking! I'll make the bed, get everything ready..." She whispered sexily.

"Ok, you win. Later..." He replied, looking at her through half closed, lust filled eyes.

By late afternoon, they had finished unpacking everything, and 'Teach an

Tobar' was feeling homely. The underfloor heating was warm enough to walk on barefooted, but they still decided to light the firepit for the first time. Shaun went outside to chop logs, as the mist rolled in from the sea and dusk fell.

They prepared dinner together, a simple pan of fresh mussels in garlic and white wine, chorizo, stuffed vine leaves and calamari, served with fresh, crusty bread they had bought on their way. They sat at the breakfast bar, on the gorgeous 'Gubi' barstools, eating their supper and drinking champagne, as darkness enveloped the house. Shaun held his glass to hers.

"To us... and this house." He said. Rebecca clinked his glass with her own and sipped the ice cold champagne.

They woke early the next morning to sunlight streaming into the bedroom, the faint calls of gulls and gannets diving for fish in the ocean. Rebecca sat up in bed, taking in the vista before her. The tide was as far out as the eye could see, the white sand beyond the dunes stretching for miles. She looked across at Shaun, who was watching her with a smile on his face.

"Like it?" He asked, as he reached for her.

"I love it... I slept so well. The sheets are gorgeous, aren't they?" she slid over to him, nestling into him, her head on his chest. He ran his hand over her breasts, watching as her nipples hardened beneath the silk.

"Yes, they are..." He said, pulling the sheet down over her hips as his lips kissed her everywhere. She felt him growing hard against her, as he rolled onto his back, pulling her on top of him. As she straddled him, he grabbed her buttocks and lifted her onto him, entering her slowly and completely. She arched her back as she rocked back and forth. He held her hips and moved with her, as they shuddered and climaxed together, the sound of the ocean in the distance.

After breakfast, they walked down to the beach. The wind was gentler than the previous day, and the sun felt warm. They cut through the dunes, with the long marram grass brushing against their legs, the fine, white sand billowing like smoke round their ankles as they walked. When they reached the beach, they turned back to look up at the house, the mountains behind it high and craggy as they reached majestically for the sky. Shaun pointed out the seabirds who would make nests in their nooks and crannies, mainly shearwater and plover birds, he told her.

"It is just so beautiful. Ireland is beautiful. It tugs at my heartstrings! I'm so happy to be here!" Rebecca beamed at him, and he pulled her to him, kissing her gently.

They carried on walking towards the sea, past the enormous caves he had taken her in before. Now the tide was so far out they were easily accessible, with giant turquoise rock-pools outside their cavernous entrances, left behind by the sea. Shaun told her about the Spanish Armada, galleons sunk off these shores three hundred years ago, and how as a boy he had found silver ducats on this very beach, washed up over centuries.

They walked for a couple of hours, by which time the briny wind off the sea was picking up and blowing their hair wildly.

"C'mon, let's head back?" Shaun shouted over the wind. They raced each other across the sand for a bit, Rebecca's heart thumping in her chest, and she realised she'd never felt freer.

Chapter 17.

Nigel.

He opened the solicitor's letter that had just landed on the doormat with a thud. Dated 7th November, it contained the *'Decree Absolut'* documents and a yellow 'post it' note stuck to it said *'please sign and return in pre- paid envelope.'*

He walked into the kitchen, now bare and cold, the only furniture a table and one chair, which he pulled out and sat down on. He leant on the table, his shoulders slumped and his head in his hands. So this was it. The end. Rebecca was finally free. Or was she? His phone buzzed, and he reached for it. No caller ID.

"Hello?"

"Mr Rodgers? Elaine here, from Simpson and Fosters. We have some good news!"

Nigel's mind went blank for a moment. Then he remembered… she was the estate agent dealing with the sale of the house.

"Yes?" He mumbled.

"We've received an offer on your property, a good one."

"What is it?" He asked.

"£750,000. And no chain!" she answered, excitement in her voice.

"Have you told my wife?" He asked.

"No, we have called you first, as you are living in the property."

"I'll speak to Mrs Rodgers. I'll get back to you." He said and hung up.

Elaine looked at the phone… how rude, she thought. Mind you, she hadn't much liked him when she went to value the house. She hadn't expected an offer like that, either... the place needed absolutely everything doing to it. Still, its location had made it extremely desirable.

Nigel emailed Rebecca, keeping it curt.

"Offer received-£750,000. I think it's a good one. Let me know immediately if you want to accept... I think so. But of course, it's your decision as well. I would have thought you can't wait to be shot of the place, now you're holed up with your fancy man. Nigel."

He slammed the laptop shut and looked at the time. Due at Stuart's in an hour, he looked around him. Most of the furniture had been got rid of. The boys' stuff was in boxes, ready for them to either collect or dispose of. A few personal belongings lay about, but mostly the house was a shell. An empty shell, ready to leave. He hadn't decided whether to move in with Stuart. Much as he wanted him to,

Nigel just wasn't sure, he valued his freedom too much. Sighing, he looked at the form in front of him.

Might as well sign it, not much point in delaying it any further, it wasn't like Rebecca was going to change her mind. He sniggered at the thought, and signed the form, pressing so hard the biro he used snapped in half.

'Teach an Tobar.'

Rebecca clicked on her emails. She saw the solicitor's one, and, opening it, she gave a whoop of joy.

"Shaun! It's here! The Decree Absolut!" she cried out. He came up behind her in the kitchen and put his arms around her waist, kissing her neck.
"Sign it." He whispered.

As she did the electronic signature, her hand was shaking. He put his own hand gently on top, to steady hers. She signed and clicked *"send"* turning around to look at him. She didn't know whether to laugh or cry.

Laugh, because she was finally free, or cry for all the wasted years. Shaun held her tightly, and they stayed like that for a few moments. The only sound was their breathing.

Later, she read the email from Nigel. She told Shaun about the offer on the house. "I think you should take it. Just get the whole thing wrapped up. Otherwise, it will be Christmas and nobody looks at property then, it could be the spring before anything happens." He said, massaging her shoulders gently.

"Yes, I agree. I'll email him back." She replied.

After dinner, they lay on the couch with the firepit lit, the clear sky just turning velvety black and stars appearing by the minute. Shaun had rigged up the Hi-Fi, and soft chill-out music filled the room. He filled her wine glass and lay back with her, as they looked out on the night.

"What a significant day." Rebecca mused.

"Indeed. We've been waiting for it, darling. Now we can plan our future. This is our beginning." He said, holding his glass to hers.

"I must talk to the boys, tell them what's going on. I don't suppose Nigel will have been in touch with them." She said, feeling a twinge of guilt.

"You mustn't feel guilty. They are grown men now, living their own lives. I'm sure they will be happy for you." Shaun said, encouragingly.

"You always make me feel better, thank you." She sighed, as she lay her head on his shoulder.

After breakfast the next morning, Shaun went to chop firewood and Rebecca called James. He answered eventually, sounding groggy.

"Hi, Mum? Is that you?" He said.

"Yes, darling. How are you?"

"Hungover! Rave last night in the student union. How are you...where are you?" He asked.

She told him all about the move, the house, telling him she would text the address, and finally that she and Nigel were officially divorced, the house under offer. There was silence as James took it all in.

"Blimey, Mum. It all seems a bit quick?" He said, eventually.

"No, it's not been quick. It's taken years, I'm sorry to say. But nothing changes how I feel about you two, you're the best sons I could ever have wished for. I hope you will come over? Maybe

Christmas?" She said, as a hard lump formed in her throat.

"I dunno Mum, Karen's folks have invited me, but it's not definite. Can I let you know?" He said, falteringly.

Rebecca said of course, and then called Sam, which was a totally different conversation.

He sobbed when she told him all the news, but eventually composed himself, and even agreed to visit at Christmas, as long as Nigel didn't object. Shaun could see how upset Rebecca was when he came back in with the firewood. He put the bucket down and hugged her.

"Shall we go for a walk? Then we can come back and have some of that amazing soup you've made." He said, brushing her tears away with his fingers.

They walked up the road this time, taking the mountain path towards the waterfall. Although it was visible from the house, it took an hour to reach. Rebecca looked up at it, cascading down the mountain with force until it reached the bottom and flowed out towards the sea.

The noise of the rushing water was deafening, too loud to talk, so they just stood, holding hands and staring up at it. The cold air had cleared her head, and as they walked back to the house, she felt calmer. There was something truly magical about this place, as if nature had put its arms around her, holding her, feeling her fragility and making her strong again.

They went to town the next day, to pick up the new car that Shaun had ordered before Rebecca had met him. Shaun drove the Dublin hire vehicle back to the car hire first, then they walked across the bustling town to the Landrover garage. People nodded and greeted Shaun, a few stopped to chat, welcoming Rebecca to the area. A couple of women made invitations for tea. She felt pleased, relieved. Her new life here had begun, and she wasn't afraid anymore.

In the garage, the salesman came over to greet them. "Mr. Forsythe! Welcome! You'll be delighted when you see your new vehicle! Come over, would you like coffee or tea?" The pretty receptionist made drinks for them while they waited for the paperwork. Rebecca noticed her looking furtively at Shaun as she placed the drinks in front of them.

"Is that you, Shaun?" she asked, shyly.

He looked at her. "Denise? I would never have recognised you!" he said, holding his hand out.

"Aye, well, you've been away a long time. I'm married with three wains now!" she said, giggling like a schoolgirl.

"This is Rebecca, my fiancée." He said, putting his arm around Rebecca's shoulders.

"Pleased to meet you. I know Shaun from school... a long time ago, now!" Denise said, looking embarrassed. "Well, Connor will be with you shortly. Nice to meet you, Rebecca." She said, leaving them to drink their coffees. Rebecca looked at Shaun, one eyebrow raised quizzically. He squeezed her hand, winking. "Later." He mouthed.

Connor reappeared and put the new car keys down on the table.

"Just a wee signature here, and here, then I'll take you outside. I think you'll be very pleased, she's a beaut." He said, as Shaun took the pen he offered, and signed.

They followed Connor outside, over to a new Landrover Discovery parked on the forecourt. He opened the drivers' door for Shaun, and as he climbed in,

Connor motioned for Rebecca to get in the other side, and then talked them through the various functions of the vehicle. Rebecca looked at Shaun. He had told her how he'd always wanted one of these, and his expression was like that of a young lad who'd just got his very first car.

Shaun drove them out of the garage, headed back on the 40 minute journey to Lough Rosslaire. The weather was perfect, dry and bright, and once they'd left the town, Shaun put his foot down and tested the car's acceleration.

"It's so smooth!" Rebecca exclaimed, as she sunk back into the leather seat.

"It's a beautiful drive, that's for sure! I'll let you have a go, if you like?" He said, excitedly. He drove on, passing landmarks that were now becoming familiar to Rebecca. Pulling over after a bit, he let Rebecca climb into the driver's seat. Finding it an easier drive than anything she'd ever experienced, they reached the house and she drove up the road to it, the four-wheel drive tackling the gravelly slope with ease.

"I am well pleased!" Shaun said as he got out. "I finally got the motor I've always wanted... and the woman I've always dreamed of!" He said, as he came around and lifted her out of the drivers' seat. "And soon, I get to carry you over this threshold!" He kissed her, pressing into her against the bonnet of the car. She kissed him back as she arched her back, thrusting her hips into him.

"And who's Denise?" she asked, as his hands crept under her jumper.

"We went out... when I was fourteen!" he laughed.

"Well, she still has the hots for you!" Rebecca said, giggling back at him.

"Ah well, that's no bother to me! I only have eyes for you, my darling." He replied, finding her breasts as he pushed her jumper up and lowered his lips to them.

The sound of a car nearby made Rebecca pull her jumper down in haste, as Shaun looked to see where it was coming from. It stopped almost as soon as they'd heard it, and then started again, but this time it faded away.

"I can't see anyone… c'mon, let's go inside, it's getting late." Shaun said, reaching for Rebecca's hand.

Nigel.

The email read:

"Hello Nigel, it is an excellent offer, and I am happy to go with it. I think it makes sense to try and get it sorted before Christmas. I will sign the paperwork as soon as I receive it.

Regards,

Rebecca."

I bet you will, you bitch, thought Nigel, as he read the email again. He dialled Simpson & Fosters, Elaine answering on the second ring.

"It's Mr. Rodgers. We accept the offer of £750,000. How long will it take to get things completed?" He demanded.

"Congratulations, Mr Rodgers. I will get in touch with the buyers and get straight back to you. How does that sound?" Elaine said, her voice quivering as she thought of her commission.

"Make it quick. Thanks." Nigel replied, hanging up.

He shut the laptop and heard his phone buzz. Stuart.

"What is it?" he said, abruptly.

"Ooh, darling. What's up with you? I was just ringing to see if you fancied going out for a drink?" Stuart replied.

"Ok, just a quick one. I'll meet you at the pub in an hour." Nigel ended the call. Damn, he really wasn't in the mood for Stuart.

Elaine called him back half an hour later, to advise him the buyers had instructed their solicitors to proceed with the sale, suggesting that Nigel should instruct his, accordingly. He acknowledged her instructions, emailed his solicitors, and left the house to meet Stuart.

As he shut the front door, he saw a van pull up, remove the "For Sale" board, and replace it with a "Sale Agreed" one. Jesus, they didn't waste much bloody time, he thought, bitterly.

Walking to the pub, his shoulders hunched against the cold, he suddenly felt uncertain of the future. He'd been able to live his secret life easily, all these years. Now what was he to do? He wouldn't be able to hide behind his own front door anymore, that was for sure. He sighed as he reached the pub. A bloody good drink, that's what he needed, he decided.

Chapter 18.

'Teach an Tobar,' one week later.

"Where shall we put the Christmas tree?" Shaun asked. "We could go for a really big one... 7ft at least?"

"That huge? Wow! If we put it by the front windows, the lights will reflect on them, it will look magical!" Rebecca said, excitedly.

A real tree! She thought of the pathetic, artificial tree she had put up every year for the last 20-odd years. Nigel had hated Christmas... unnecessary expense and a complete waste of time, he'd always said. He'd even complained about the amount Rebecca spent on the festive food. But she always made the best of it for the boys. She didn't think they'd been aware of his meanness... she'd always over-compensated and they never went without, however much he moaned.

Shaun drove out to a nearby farm that they'd noticed a few days before, advertising Xmas trees. Choosing a fabulous 7ft one, Shaun fixed it to the roof rack. On their way back, he pulled in at 'Mcgettigan's' department store, and Rebecca dashed in to get lights, baubles, decorations and a tree stand.

Back at the house, they carried the tree in between them, and stood it by the windows at the front of the living room. As they pulled the netting off, the tree revealed itself in all its true glory. The smell of fresh pine needles filled the air, and Rebecca shivered with pleasure. That afternoon, they decorated it together and as it grew dark outside they switched the lights on and stood back to admire their handiwork.

"It looks gorgeous! I'm so excited!" Rebecca jumped up and down, as Shaun grabbed hold of her and pulled her to the couch. He lay on top of her whispering, "This will be the best Christmas ever!" He bent to kiss her as she wrapped her arms around him and pulled him closer.

Rebecca heard her phone beep and reached for it, checking the screen. It was a text message from her solicitor, asking her to call. She sighed as she sat up and dialled the number.

"It's Rebecca… Rodgers." She stuttered, remembering she could now use her maiden name.

"Ah, good afternoon, Susan Clark speaking. I just wanted to let you know, exchange has already taken place on your property, with completion expected within the next two weeks, the buyers want to be in by Christmas, isn't that splendid news?"

"Yes... yes, really good news. Is Mr. Rodgers aware?" Rebecca asked.

"I've sent him a message, but he hasn't responded. Please could you send me an encrypted email with your bank details, so we can transfer the funds? Although that may not be until after Christmas."

"Yes, I will do that straight away, thank you." Rebecca replied.

"Thank you, have a lovely Christmas."

Shaun opened a bottle of Laurent Perrier, and they sat by the tree, its lights twinkling prettily in the darkness.

"So, I'm really free of everything that held me, now." She said as she sipped her champagne.

"Yes, and we're going to have a wonderful Christmas, darling. Here's to it." Shaun held his glass to hers, and kissed her, and as she responded, tasting the sweetness of the champagne on his lips.

That night, they were woken up by a cars' bright headlights, shining up at the windows from outside. Shaun reached for his watch as Rebecca stirred beside him.

"Who the devil is that, out here at this time?" he said, his voice groggy. "It's 3am!"

The lights faded away as Shaun got up to look out of the windows. He could just make out the cars' taillights, driving off. He climbed back into bed, reaching for Rebecca.

"Strange. Nobody comes out here, much, especially not this time in the morning. They must have been lost." He snuggled back into her, and they went back to sleep.

They awoke to a thick, freezing fog. It completely obscured the view from all the windows. "Ugh! What a horrible day!" Rebecca said, as she contemplated a day spent inside, which she didn't mind at all. She'd make a start on her Christmas cake, maybe make some mince pies, too. They could take some round to Bridget and Liam's later if the fog cleared, she thought.

"I've a bit of work to do, are you ok on your own for a bit?" Shaun asked, as he kissed her neck from behind.

"Yes, I'm going to do some baking. Do you think this will clear?" she asked, hopefully.

"Yes, should be gone by 3 or 4 o'clock. Why's that, darling?"

"I thought we could drop some mince pies round to Bridget's, I need some groceries anyway, and it's on the way?"

"Lovely idea, maybe text her, let her know?" Shaun suggested.

Rebecca tied her hair up, put her apron on, and got to work in the kitchen. As she was rolling out the pastry for the mince pies, she heard a sound from outside. "Shaun? Is that you?" she called. She walked over to the back door and looked out through the glass. Hearing a car door shut in the distance, she opened the door. Stepping outside, she noticed the fog had lifted slightly, and she could hear the hum of an engine, then she saw red taillights driving away from the house, at the bottom of the hill.

She ran back into the house and went into the living room where Shaun was at his desk.

"Did you hear that?" she asked, but then she saw he had his air pods in. He took them out when he saw her.

"Are you ok darling? What is it?" He asked, looking alarmed.

"There was a car, again. Right down there, at the bottom of the drive. And I heard a sound outside. I'm scared, Shaun."

"Let me finish up here, then we can go for a drive, see if anything looks suspicious on the road... will you be ready in an hour or so? We can stop at Bridget's, and then the Spar after, ok?" He said.

"Ok, I'll just finish making the mince pies to take with us."

Later, they left the house, Shaun taking the road very carefully. There were pockets of fog still obscuring it in places.

"Are you worried?" she asked him.

"It is weird, but it could just be someone lost, or out for a drive. I don't know. It's so remote out here, it's easy enough to lose your bearings, so it is." Shaun squeezed her hand.

"It's the third time we've heard it, though." Rebecca said, feeling uneasy.

They got to Bridget's, and she made them tea. Delighted with the mince pies Rebecca presented her with, she exclaimed, "And they are still warm! God bless you, dear."

"Now, how are you settling in? Liam and I are looking forward to coming over for a visit!" she said.

"Why don't you come this Saturday? We can have Christmas drinks?" Rebecca suggested.

"I'll check with Liam, I'm sure that'll be fine! What time?" Bridget replied.

"Early, Brig. You'll want to see the place in the light, and the roads aren't great after dark, as you well know." Shaun said.

They left Bridget's, stopped at the supermarket where Rebecca picked up a few supplies, and headed back home.

Daylight was just fading, the shortest day not far off, now.

"Take care, Shaun. It's still really foggy." Rebecca said, as they set off for Lough Rosslaire.

"Aye, but the lights on this are grand, see?" He said, as the rear fog lights illuminated at the touch of a button on the digital display.

They reached the fork in the main road, turning left for the track that led to the house. Suddenly, the fog became much thicker, and Shaun could barely make out the road ahead. Then, out of nowhere, two bright headlights appeared behind, coming closer and closer, blinding Shaun's rear vision.

"Jesus, what the fuck?" he exclaimed, as the car got nearer, until it was right up close to the back of the Discovery.

"What is it? What's happening?" Rebecca shrieked. Shaun slammed his foot on the brakes and the car behind swerved violently, veering off the road, out of control, and smashed into a boulder at the side of the road.

"Oh my God! Oh my God, Shaun!" Rebecca screamed.

They could just make out the driver, slumped forward, their head must have hit the horn, as it was blasting out continuously. Then the car burst into flames.

Shaun revved the engine, backing the Landrover into a fast reverse, away from the fire, which had now taken hold of the other car.

"We have to help them, Shaun! We can't just let them burn to death!" Rebecca was crying hysterically now.

"Call the Garda, quickly!" Shaun threw his phone at her, and somehow, her hands shaking uncontrollably, she managed to call 112. Shaun jumped out of the car, running towards the burning vehicle. As he got nearer, the intensity of the flames grew, the acrid smoke stinging his eyes. He tried to get to the driver, but the flames were too intense now. He knew it was too dangerous to get any nearer, and backed away, fearful of an explosion.

"Emergency, what is the problem?" a voice asked.

"There's a car on fire, someone's inside!" Rebecca shouted down the phone.

"What's the location please?"

"Lough Rosslaire, the sea road... the road that leads down to the beach... please, quickly!"

"Sending Garda and Fire now. Please hold the line."

Within what seemed like minutes, the sirens were audible and blue flashing lights appeared before them, just visible in the dense fog. Garda, a fire engine, an ambulance. The car hadn't exploded, but was now nothing but a burning wreck, thick black smoke emanating from it.

Rebecca sat in the Landrover, sobbing softly as Shaun placed his arm around her.

"They're dead, aren't they? It's too late." She cried.

"Yes, I'm afraid it is." Shaun hugged her tighter.

They sat in the car as the emergency services dealt with the scene. An officer came over to them, to ask for their version of what had happened. Shaun gave him all the information he could, mentioning the suspicious movements of a car in the area, over the last couple of days. When the officer had finished taking notes, he told them they could go, and that someone would contact them in the next few days. As Shaun drove on towards the house, Rebecca looked back, still sobbing.

Shaun poured them a brandy each, and they sat, arms round each other looking out into the night sky, a bluish glow still visible from the lights at the scene of the accident. Rebecca could smell the smoke on him, in his hair and on his skin. She stroked his face gently, as she whispered, "you could have been hurt."

"There was nothing I could do. But whoever it was in that car was definitely following us. It must be the same car that's been hanging around, the last couple of days." Shaun stood up. "I'm going to take a shower, will you be ok for a bit?" he said.

"Yes, I'm ok. I'll get dinner ready." She replied.

Rebecca kept herself busy in the kitchen, trying not to think of the awful incident that afternoon. Realising she felt nervous now, alone in the kitchen with nothing but darkness outside, she put the tv on for company. The local news was on, and a reporter was covering the accident. She opened the back door and looked out, and, sure enough, there was an RTE van down where the accident had happened, the burnt-out shell of a car now being removed from the scene by a tow truck. She shut the door and turned back to the tv, increasing the volume to hear the reporter's commentary.

"We now know that the male driver, not believed to be a local man, died in the car, which crashed and caught fire at approximately 4.10pm today. The car, which had Dublin number-plates, was a Volkswagen Golf. Garda are appealing for witnesses, other than the two people that were interviewed at the scene. Rescue services have removed the car for further forensic investigation."

Rebecca ran to the stairs, calling up for Shaun. He came out onto the landing, looking worried.

"What is it?" he asked, as he dried himself off.

"The fire... a man died, not local, they don't think! It had Dublin plates... a Golf!" she said, frantically.

He came down the stairs slowly and took her in his arms.

"Turn the tv off, let's try not to think about it for a while, darling."

She sobbed into his damp shoulder, smelling the fresh scent of shower gel and after shave. He kissed her gently and wiped the tears from her cheeks.

Rebecca slept fitfully that night, images of a burnt corpse in a car wreck appearing in her dreams. Waking up several times hoping it *was* all just a bad dream, then realising it wasn't, she eventually got up and went downstairs.

Dawn was just breaking with the promise of a beautiful day.

She made tea and sat drinking it by the huge window at the front, wrapping herself in a fur throw. The sky was shot with streaks of pink and orange, and gulls hovered on the wind, eagerly looking for breakfast. Such beauty all around, yet now it seemed tainted with the horror of yesterday's accident. Sighing, she rubbed her eyes to try and erase the memory of it.

Shaun came down to find her asleep on the couch. He sat beside her, stroking her head, as she stirred and opened her eyes.

"Oh, I fell asleep! I had such a terrible night and came down here early to make a drink." She said, pulling him closer to her.

"I know you did, you were tossing and turning all night. Let's get out for a long walk on the beach after breakfast, it might help clear our heads?" He suggested.

He made toast and more tea, while Rebecca showered and got dressed. They left the house, deliberately walking in the opposite direction, so as not to see the site of the accident.

They reached the beach and walked right along it, to its furthest point. The tide was miles out, and the sun was shining. For December, it was a mild day. As they headed back, Rebecca's phone buzzed in her pocket. She took it out and saw a text from Sam.

"Hi Mum, hope you're ok. I've been trying to get hold of Dad, I wanted to know what he's doing for Xmas before I decide what I'm going to do, but he's not answering. I've left him voicemails and texted him twice. Let me know if you hear from him? Xx"

She showed Shaun the text.

"I should try calling him, I think?" she said.

"Yes, probably, it will put Sam's mind at rest if you can get hold of him. Why not wait till we're back at the house?"

"Ok, good idea." Rebecca put the phone back in her pocket, and they walked back along the beach, as the tide slowly started rolling in.

Nigel, one week earlier.

Stuart handed him a pint of beer, as Nigel sat down opposite him in the pub.

"What's up?" he asked.

"House is sold. She's getting half. And I'm to be homeless. That's what." He said bitterly, downing half the beer in one go.

"I've told you, you can move in with me. I know it's only a council flat, but it'll do, won't it? Then we can make plans?"

"Plans? What plans?" asked Nigel.

"Plans for our future! I thought that's what you wanted?" Stuart asked, feeling uncertainty creeping in.

"I don't know what I want. But I do know, she can't just walk away like this. I want her to suffer, and him. Why should she move on, smelling of roses? Bitch. That's what she is, a selfish bitch." Nigel finished his beer, his face becoming flushed with anger.

"Look, mate, you've got to leave it behind. Ain't going to do you no good being like this." Stuart said, sadly. This wasn't what he'd expected at all.

Nigel stood up to leave. "I'll call you." He said, as he turned on his heel and left the pub.

Back at the house, he texted James, and then sent the same text to Sam:

"Hi mate. Can you text me your Mother's new address, please? I want to send a Christmas card. Thanks, Dad."

As he waited for one of them to respond, he poured himself a whiskey, got out his laptop, and booked a Ryan Air flight to Dublin for the following day.

Chapter 19.

'Teach an Tobar.'

The front doorbell rang, and Shaun went to answer it. Two uniformed Garda were outside.

"May we come in? We'd like to speak to Mrs. Rodgers, please?" one of them said.

"Of course, please do." Shaun stood aside and let them in. Rebecca was in the kitchen. He led them through and when she heard their voices, she turned towards them, feeling her heart race as she saw the two officers standing before her.

"Mrs. Rodgers, we are sorry to inform you that we have reason to believe the body in the car fire two days ago was that of your husband, Mr. Nigel Rodgers."

Rebecca's hands flew to her face as she gasped for breath. Shaun quickly went to her and put his arm around her for support.

"My fiancée is divorced, Mr. Rodgers was her ex-husband, as of a couple of weeks ago." He explained to the officers.

"How... how do you know it was him?" she asked, in a weak voice.

"We traced the car back to where it was hired, and they confirmed the name and address given, the UK address. We contacted the British police, and it seems Mr Rodgers had been reported missing, by a Mr. Sam Rodgers, two days ago, and also by a Mr. Stuart Cameron?" the Garda confirmed.

"We cannot ask you to identify the body, for obvious reasons, so we are relying on dental records for that, if you could give us contact details for your ex-husbands' dentist?" He added.

Rebecca felt her legs buckling beneath her, and sat down on a barstool, her head in her hands.

"Yes, I will get you those details. Who... is Stuart Cameron? And... has anyone contacted my sons? Sam is one of them..." she asked.

"We were rather hoping you could tell us who Mr. Cameron is? And no, we thought it best if you contact your sons."

"No, I can't tell you...I don't know the name at all." She replied, frantically scrolling her contacts for the dentist's number. When she'd given them the contact details, they said they would be in touch and turned to leave. Shaun showed them out and came back into the kitchen, taking Rebecca in his arms.

"I must phone the boys." She whispered, her voice shaking.

Rebecca's hands trembled as she dialled Sam's number. She took a deep breath as he answered the call on the third ring.

"Mum... is that you?" Sam said, sounding worried.

"Yes, darling. Sam, there has been a terrible accident, involving your father."

"What! What's happened? Mum?" Sam's voice became frantic.

"He was here, in Ireland. Two days ago. He was following us, and there was a terrible fog. His car swerved into an enormous boulder and caught fire, Sam. He didn't survive, I'm so sorry, darling." She felt her throat constrict as Sam started wailing down the phone.

"No Mum, no, no, no! It can't be true! Please, no!" he cried.

Shaun rubbed her shoulders as she tried to offer Sam some sort of consolation, but eventually he ended the call, unable to speak any longer, and then she tried James' number.

That call was equally devastating, James demanding more information than Sam had, until Rebecca said she needed to rest, and that she would call him later. She lay on the bed, staring out to sea, the sky as bleak and angry as she felt. Shaun brought her paracetamol and a glass of water. She took two, and fell back into the pillows, looking at him sorrowfully.

"He followed me here, he wanted to spoil things for us, I know it. And he has..." she whispered.

"No, he hasn't, Rebecca. You mustn't let that thought corrupt your mind. We will be okay, we have each other. We have made our home here, and we won't let anything spoil that, ever." Shaun took her in his arms, stroking her head gently. Eventually, she lay back and slept, a deep, dreamless sleep.

Chapter 20.

Christmas Day.

"This is for you, Mum." Sam handed her a neatly wrapped box, tied with a red satin ribbon. She untied the ribbon and lifted the lid off the box. Inside was a smaller box, and when she opened that, she saw a beautiful silver Celtic cross necklace, inlaid with a heart-shaped mother-of-pearl stone, which had an iridescent, creamy glow.

"Oh Sam, it's gorgeous! How thoughtful of you, darling!"

"Do you like it? Shaun helped me choose it. He told me the meaning of it." Sam said, earnestly.

"And tell me, what is that?" Rebecca asked, as she lifted her hair, and Shaun fastened it around her neck. As it settled onto her collarbone, he stroked the four arms of the cross on the pendant.

"Four ways to ascension. An invitation to know God, nature, wisdom and the self. The circles around the intersection of the cross represent unification, totality, wholeness and inclusion. It is seen as a meeting place of divine energies, a symbolic compass, if you like, offering spiritual navigation." Shaun explained.

"I'll never take it off, thank you, Sam." She hugged him tightly as she felt tears welling in her eyes.

"That's ok, Mum. I wanted to get you something meaningful, and... healing."

After eating a delicious lunch that they'd all had a hand in preparing, they went out for a walk. It was late afternoon, the sun just sinking on the horizon. Sam had asked to see where the accident had happened, so they walked slowly down the road towards the boulder that marked the spot.

Rebecca had left a small bunch of snowflakes there the day before.

They stood in silence. Sam closed his eyes, and took a deep breath, as Rebecca held the cross around her neck, gently feeling its four prongs. Shaun put his arm around her and kissed her head.

"It's a shame James couldn't come." Sam mumbled.

"I know, darling, but he had already committed himself to Karen's parents. We'll all be together next week, at the funeral."

They walked down to the beach, as the sky was turning a beautiful shade of salmon pink, tinged with purple, and Rebecca thought of an old quote:

"No sun outlasts its sunset,

But it will rise again, to see the dawn."

Richmond, Surrey.

Nigel's funeral was being held at 11 am, at Mortlake Crematorium. Shaun, Rebecca and Sam had arrived the day before, and were staying at the Kings Head pub, where the reception was to be held afterwards. They headed to the service after a late breakfast, and as they reached the entrance gates, James was waiting there for them.

He hugged Rebecca, and Sam, silently. Then he shook Shaun's hand, and turned to introduce his girlfriend, Karen.

"I'm sorry to meet you under such sad circumstances." She said, softly.

The ceremony was brief, with James reading a poem he had written for Nigel, and the minister conducting a brief eulogy about Nigel that the boys had written, together. Rebecca noticed a man across the aisle that she didn't recognise and was surprised to see that he was weeping. Afterwards, as they congregated outside, the man came over to Rebecca and Shaun.

"You must be Rebecca?" he asked quietly.

"Yes, I am, and this is Shaun. And you are...?"

"Stuart... Cameron. I was a good mate of Nigel's. We had an arrangement, and he didn't show up. That's when I reported him missing, as I'd been unable to get hold of him for a couple of days. I read what had happened, in the local paper. I'm so sorry for your loss." He shook Rebecca's hand and turned to walk away.

"Wait!" she called. "Please come back to the King's Head, there are refreshments?"

"Thank you, that's kind." He nodded and turned away again.

Chapter 21.

France, six months later.

A string quartet played as the waiters walked amongst the guests, offering delicate canapes and champagne on silver trays. The hot afternoon sun was high in the sky, and a huge white gazebo offered welcome shelter for the guests who had congregated to attend the wedding.

When the pastor arrived, Kath welcomed him, showing him to the table and chairs set up beneath another gazebo, where the wedding ceremony was to take place. Strategically placed stone urns overflowed with pale pink peonies, lily of the valley, and highly perfumed stocks. Kath's beloved wind chimes hung from tree branches, tinkling as the gentle breeze blew them together.

Bob knocked quietly on the door of the annexe.

"Are you ready, darling? It's nearly time!" he said, nervously.

"She's nearly ready, Dad!" Andrea answered.

Rebecca stood up, smoothing out her dress, as Andrea positioned her veil.

"Perfect, you look perfect, sis!" she smiled, as a tear slipped down her cheek.

Rebecca took one last look at herself in the long mirror. Her ivory Grecian style crepe de chine dress by Ghost was absolutely breath-taking in its simplicity, and moulded to her curves, flatteringly. A pearl headband held her veil, a fine silk tulle, in place. It complemented the pearl Celtic cross that she never took off.

She wore her parents' 21st birthday diamond earrings, and Andrea had given her a blue aquamarine brooch, which she had pinned to her bra. Her most extravagant purchase had been the Jimmy Choo satin kitten heels, which she stepped into, and finally she was ready to marry the man of her dreams, as she took the bouquet of white lily of the valley flowers Andrea held out for her.

Bob took an intake of breath when he saw her.

"You look lovely, my dear. Come on." He held his arm out to her, and they walked towards the gazebo, the string quartet playing Pachelbel's Canon, as Andrea followed behind them.

There were gasps from the guests, as Rebecca walked in between them to the front of the gazebo. Shaun turned to look at her as she took her place beside him. He reached for her hand, smiling.

"You are beautiful." He whispered. He wore a cream linen suit, with a pale blue cravat. His tanned skin made his eyes a brighter shade of blue, and his dark hair was slicked back. She smiled back at him. "Thank you, darling." She whispered back.

The pastor conducted the ceremony mostly in heavily accented English, until the very end when, after Shaun had slipped a Tiffany's platinum wedding band on to Rebecca's finger and she had done the same with his, he smiled and said:

"Vous pouvez maintenant embrasser la mariée."

Shaun lifted Rebecca's veil and bent to kiss her, as the guests broke into a rapturous applause.

The servers lay the wedding banquet out on long tables dressed with antique white linen, candles and sprigs of lily of the valley, benches either side.

Guests tucked into caviar, prawns, mussels and lobster to begin, followed by a hog roast, basted with Bob's 'secret' marinade. Champagne flowed, and a Gipsy Kings tribute band replaced the string quartet, as the afternoon heat turned into a cooler evening with a gentle breeze, stars appearing in the violet twilight sky.

Friends and family crowded around as Shaun and Rebecca took to the dancefloor, surrounded by candles, for their first dance. The band played "She" by Charles Aznavour, which Shaun had chosen, saying it epitomised his feelings for Rebecca.

Lucy and Mia cried as they watched the newly-weds dancing. Jackie and Alan held hands and swayed to the music as they looked on, glad that Rebecca had at last found the happiness that she so deserved.

Andrea danced with Harry, and they decided they should renew their vows.

Molly and Jack watched them, pleased they weren't arguing for once.

James and Karen, who had recently got engaged, decided they wanted their wedding to be just like this one.

Sam, though still single, had been getting on quite well with Lucy. She was slightly older than him, but he didn't mind that... and she was a talented dancer.

Bridget and Liam, who had never been to France, relished every moment of the occasion, delighted that the brothers, Joe and Fergal, had both been able to make the trip over from the US.

Declan got on well with Shaun's relatives and promised to visit when back in Ireland. Aunt Norah had also made the journey over and seemed to be enjoying Declan's company.

Kath and Bob, who had overseen the wedding planning and all the arrangements sat watching the proceedings, as they toasted each other, overwhelmed with happiness for Rebecca after all she had been through.

Chapter 22.

'Teach an Tobar.'

Rebecca turned over, taking in the comforting sight of Shaun asleep next to her. How far they had come on their journey, she thought. She would never have believed fate would intervene in the way it had.

Dawn was just breaking, the morning sun trying to emerge from the dark sky night had left behind, golden rays appearing as the buffeting wind moved the clouds. How she loved it here, in Ireland. The scenery that changed so dramatically, day by day, hour by hour, and the inner peace she had found since moving here.

She smiled as she heard Pooky calling for her from the bottom of the stairs. Pooky, her cocker spaniel, a wedding present from Shaun. The little dog never left her side and had proved to be an amusing companion in her life, especially when Shaun was away, or working in his study. She went downstairs to make tea, and Pooky stopped barking immediately, as her tail wagged in excitement. Rebecca bent down and snuggled into her neck.

"Good morning, Pooks! What have you been up to?" she laughed as the dog cocked her head and looked at Rebecca, inquisitively.

Rebecca opened the back door and let her out. As she turned back into the kitchen, she noticed her phone was buzzing. She looked at the screen, which read:

"Buncragga Wellness Resort."

"Hello?" she answered.

"Is that Mrs. Rodgers? It is Vanya, we met you here at our wellness retreat last year."

"Well, it is me, but I'm not Mrs. Rodgers anymore! How can I help?"

"We are looking to introduce a new skincare brand to the spa, and the owners want something completely organic. I remembered you telling me about the Australian brand you used and also worked for. I wondered if you would be able to come and talk to us about it?"

"Oh, Dark Rain? I see! Well, my circumstances have changed since then, I don't work for that company anymore, but I still use their products. I could certainly come and talk to you about the range... I live here, in Ireland now." She replied, thinking quickly about this proposal.

"That would be great. Let us know when you are free to come?" said Vanya.

"I will, thank you for the call."

Rebecca let Pooky back in as she made the tea. Taking one up to Shaun, she sat on the edge of the bed as he stirred.

"Morning, Mrs. Forsythe. Did I hear voices?" he asked, raising himself up on one elbow.

She told him about the call, as he drank his tea.

"Well, might as well go and see them, if you want to? Is it something you want to get back into, selling the products?"

"I don't know, I kind of feel that would be returning to my old life, you know?" she said, pensively.

"Yes, I know what you mean. And you don't need to work, you know that darling?" he said, stroking her hand.

"I know, but I *need* to do something. Maybe I should try my hand at writing. I've always wanted to, and here, with the peace and the solitude, I think it would be really possible?" Rebecca said, realising that now she had actually said it, that was what she wanted to do, more than anything.

Shaun sat up, the sheet falling and revealing his lean, tanned torso that she loved so much. He put his tea down and reached for her.

"Well, y'know I'll support everything you do, my love."

He kissed her, gently then more intensely, as he slipped her robe from her shoulders, and pulled her towards him.

THE END.

The Lake Isle of Innisfree.

I will arise and go now, and go to Innisfree,

And a small cabin build there, of clay and wattles made:

Nine bean-rows will I have there, a hive for the honey-bee;

And live alone in the bee-loud glade.

And I shall have some peace there, for peace comes dropping slow,

Dropping from the veils of the morning to where the cricket sings;

There midnight's all a glimmer, and noon a purple glow,

And evening full of the linnet's wings.

I will arise and go now, for always night and day

I hear lake water lapping with low sounds by the shore;

While I stand on the roadway, or on the pavements grey,

I hear it in the deep heart's core.

W.B.Yeats-1865-1939

Thank you for reading "The House on the Hill." I hope you have enjoyed this story, and I would be grateful if you could post a review on Amazon. It really helps other readers when deciding what to read, and means everything to the Author who wrote it.

Do connect with me on Facebook and Instagram!

Made in the USA
Middletown, DE
08 April 2021